MW00973166

"The 13 talented authors of **Many Paths, Many Feet** take you on a journey that has been a part of women's lives since Biblical times. A journey filled with challenges, victories, faith and love. A journey that motivates you to keep running when you think you can't, to keep hoping when things appear hopeless and to keep dreaming when your world is falling apart. Each experience within the pages of **Many Paths, Many Feet** will impel you to embrace your own personal journey with an even stronger determination to act on your passions and live life to its full potential."

-----Elaine Burthéy, LIFE COACH, KIBOU COACHING, LLC

"I liked the fact that this collection of stories covered a range of situations and emotions. It reminds me of a book *"Breaking Ice: An Anthology of Contemporary African-American Fiction."* The writers had different styles which made this anthology stand out."

-----Tamara Holmes, WRITER/EDITOR

"Absolutely wonderful and unique...a book made for constant use...a companion for life. Filled with love and wisdom and written in a beautifully simple, yet powerful poetic style. There is so much spirit and passion in the stories and poems that makes **Many Paths, Many Feet** a book to be savored. Give this book to everyone you care about."

-----Robert Moment, LIFE COACH, AUTHOR

"I enjoyed everything about the book, most of all the time taken by this group of professional women to put their thoughts together...I say it is a brilliant idea! Their style is unique, their talent is to be cherished and I commend them all."

-----Violet Matthew, DISTRICT SALES MANAGER, AVON

"I really enjoyed the transparency of the authors. Some of the stories were pretty raw as far as what they shared but I liked that because it made them real. There is a unique flair that other books don't have and I also think it could bring forth sequel books."

-----Kim Enfield, NEW PRAGUE, MINNESOTA

"*Many Paths, Many Feet* is a book of outstanding quality, full of short stories that have real inspirational value and are derived from common problems in life. It deserves a place on the shelf of the seasoned reader who appreciates the uplifting power of a good story."

-----Dimitrios P. Kontoyiannis, MD

Many *Paths*, Many *Feet*

An Anthology of Women's Stories

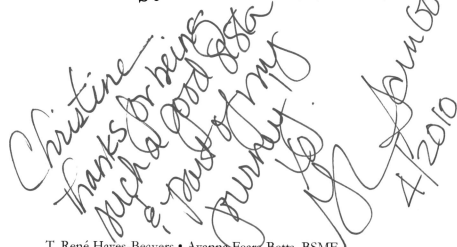

T. René Hayes-Beavers • Ayanna Fears-Betts, BSME

R. Nicole Cutts, PhD • Quenzette Jackson • Paula Jemison, MA

Verlalia Lewis, MBA • Rosalee R. Martin, PhD

Lynnell R. Morrison • Salli Y. Saxton • Gloria J. Scruggs

Lynn Simpson, MBA • Sandra Thomas, MA • Phyllis Wilson, MS

Copyright © 2010 by Phyllis Wilson

ISBN: 978-0-557-33443-8

All Rights Reserved

Printed in the United States of America

9 8 7 6 5 4 3 2 1

Acknowledgments

Many Paths, Many Feet has a lot to do with the journey, but it also has everything to do with the many people who touched each author– from our supporters, our families and friends who cheered us along the paths. We would like to express our SINCERE gratitude to all those who gave us encouragement and hope for the possibility to complete this life-changing event. This book would not have been possible without their love, friendship, wisdom and encouragement. You believed in the potential of our words contained in this collection and helped spread the message that perseverance **AND** faith is all it takes!

We are deeply indebted to Sandra Thomas whose stimulating suggestions and encouragement helped us in all the editing of our works.

Last, but certainly foremost, we would like to give thanks to God whose patient love enabled each of us to complete this work and share our experience of the various paths He has laid out for us.

Road Map

INSPIRE

PRAISE

UNITE

REFLECT

Author Profiles

Preface

In collaborating on this anthology, Many Paths, Many Feet was developed virtually by 13 women who decided to trust and share their stories under the same cover. This began as a challenge from a publisher who doubted that 13 busy women could come together to produce a work like this.

I had the distinct pleasure of taking a short stop in Houston, Texas on my journey in life to meet some phenomenal women. Little did I know that my stop would evolve into the manifestation of this book! It was during this stop that I encountered four major life changing tiles: I was inspired, I united with others toward a common goal; I began to fully understand the praise of a Higher Being and I reflected on the entire process as a necessary part of who I am.

Inspiration came in the form of words like "I have a story to share"; "I would like to help you make that vision a reality!" I used the words of enthusiasm and comments to formulate and reformulate what you hold in your hands today. To be inspired can take many forms and as you will read in the following stories and poems, being inspired requires more than just putting words to paper. It requires one to heed the small voice that beckons each one of us to move towards a greater existence.

Unity is alive and well, as I saw evidence of that fact within the women who shared in my journey. We were bonded through friendship, yet we preserved because we had an unbinding respect for the need of the feminine spirit to be exalted for all to read and understand. This anthology shows the unbridled, yet cohesiveness of our spirits.

Praise has made the journey a celebration of many sorts as sometimes the journey can be laborious but I have found God's unwavering hand always there to grasp as I struggled with the many directions our path was turning. This collection resounds with renewed spirits and accolades to living a life of gratitude.

Reflection provides an opportunity to rest and see how far we have come on a journey. It is here that we can see the workings of praise, unity and inspiration, all coupled in a peaceful spot. We took moments to breathe and sigh at the magnificence of our journeys. This section of the book provides you with time to just say "ahh."

Many Paths, Many Feet is a journey where everyone can step in and out of each other's stories for encouragement and motivation. You can find something you can relate to in each of these stories…and my hope is that each story can ultimately engender hope.

Phyllis Wilson

Inspire

My Haven

By Verlalia Lewis, MBA

I believe there's a place within me that won't let me die,

No matter what I say or do, it beckons me to try.

And strive I do, on my daily path,

To live victoriously without malice or wrath.

With every step taken I courageously sigh,

Knowing with self-confidence and faith my goals are satisfied.

But when the challenges prove fierce and I feel I should cry,

I run back to that place that won't let me die!

Never Give Up Your Quest for Life

By Verlalia Lewis, MBA

The world becomes a wondrous place,

When you allow your fear to flee.

You evaluate universal time and space,

And search for who you need to be.

Your eyes begin to truly see, not just view,

Your mind envisions endless flight,

Your heart palpitates its beat anew,

Exploring new meaning and soaring to new heights.

So never, ever give up your quest for life,

And never let the fires of passion die.

Always live for what's just and right,

But don't forget to ask the question why?

Bird Song

By Paula Jemison, M.A.

As is the norm during that time of the year, the sky was clear on that chilly March morning in Houston. It was getting close to her nesting time and Songbird, a dove, was flying high in the sky looking for the perfect spot to build her nest. She didn't have much time. If only that big loud machine hadn't come and torn down their home and frightened everyone away--the rabbits, the wrens and swallows; even the rats. One day she was settling into her perfect nest she had just built and now she's looking for another home. Songbird wasted no time moving forward because she was ready to nest.

As Songbird soared high above the area where she had lived for a decade, all she could see was cleared areas where large clusters of oak trees once stood tall. She could have migrated to the place she heard about that was a utopia for birds, but this is where she was hatched and she didn't want to go anywhere else. Besides, it wasn't that bad. She knew she needed to find a tree or area close to the ground to make it easier for her and mate her Strongfeather to search for food and not be too far from the chicks once they hatched.

As this mother bird was searching for a place to lay her eggs, a human mother was searching for a job. Little did they know they would play a pivotal role in each other lives---one that would change those lives forever.

"So can you give me an example of a time when you were faced with a team member complaining about your performance?" the woman interviewing Keisha asked. While thinking of a suitable answer to give, Keisha was trying to figure out what prompted this question. Had there been a conflict between the current team and the person who left the position she was interviewing for? That's what she didn't need--to work with a company that had internal conflict between team members. In spite of her apprehension Keisha answered with a finessed response that depicted her as a positive team player.

As Keisha finished her interview, she was secretly hoping she did not get a call-back from this company. The interviewer was too consumed with checking off all of the questions on her interview form instead of actually listening to and acknowledging Keisha's skills and qualifications for the position. Even though she desperately needed a job, finding the right fit was most important. And this particular job was entry level and Keisha was overqualified. Even though she had 15 years experience in corporate communications, she had been without a job for almost a year and her unemployment was running out. She was behind on her car payments, didn't know how she was going to pay her rent or utilities, food was scarce and her twins, Kerrin and Kyle, seemed to be growing out of their clothes overnight. She needed a job ASAP!

When Keisha arrived home, she felt drained and totally helpless. She dragged herself inside and changed to go to the grocery store to pick up a few items. While waiting in the checkout line, two young ladies in front of her were talking. One was visibly bruised and was explaining what had happened. "Girl, I can't believe he had the audacity to hit me because I told him he had to leave! I tried to knock the crap out of him and then he went ballistic. Afterwards, he tried to explain that he only hit me because he didn't want to leave. Can you believe that?" Keisha couldn't help but feel empathy for the young lady and anger towards the guy who hit her. "What kind of man hits a woman?" she thought to herself. She had been in the same situation and to see it again through someone else's eyes made her remember a pain she tried so hard to forget.

As Keisha started preparing dinner, the conversation she heard between the two women still haunted her. She tried to keep herself busy by helping the kids with their homework and even transplanted an ivy plant to a larger pot. She cleaned off her patio and hung the plant there. It looked nice hanging up on the patio and it definitely gave her sanctuary, (that's what she called her patio) a more tranquil feel like a garden. "Just what I needed," Keisha smiled to herself.

But that night, the ghosts of her past paid her a visit and reminded her how lucky she was despite her current situation. Keisha's mind recaptured the whole scene as if the years of trying to forget and months of therapy never occurred.

The kids' dad was on a tirade that night. It wasn't like he hadn't done it before. For four years she had taken his abuse. A punch in the back because she talked while he was on the phone. A slap in the face while holding one of the babies because she didn't ask him permission to rent a movie. The abuse was frequent and was getting worse every day, but this particular night she couldn't take it anymore. He picked her up from work and before she could fasten her seatbelt, he started calling her names and telling her she had something to hide because she hadn't left her work phone number where anyone in the house could find it. She tried to tell him that she put it on the refrigerator, but he kept going on and on. That's when he hit her against her head so hard that it hit the side of the car window. He parked the truck and told her to write her work phone number on a postcard ten times, while he went to have coffee inside the restaurant where they were parked. He also told her they wouldn't leave until she did it. Keisha felt helpless, scared and mad as hell. She knew she had to leave. The next day she went to work and gave her two weeks notice, explaining everything to her supervisor. She was embarrassed, but it didn't matter any longer. The only thing that mattered was that she had to leave before she had a nervous breakdown or worst, he killed her or she killed him. Two weeks later, on a cold, rainy February night she left with her two small kids. That night, just as always, he left to get coffee. This is when Keisha made her escape. She left him many times before, but this time in her heart, she knew she wouldn't return. After she left, oh he tried to get her to come back. He even had the audacity to say it was her fault that he hit her. But there was no way she would go back to someone like him or allow another man to hit her again!

Even though that event happened ten years ago, that night Keisha cried into her pillow from the hurt that she allowed him to cause her. She cried hard and intensely because she could never understand how a man who confessed his love to a woman could use his hands to hurt her so badly. She cried for the young woman she saw at the store as much as she cried for herself because she knew that if the young lady didn't break the cycle like she did, she would always find herself in abusive relationships. Or worse---she could end up dead like so many others. She also cried for her daughter and prayed that her child would never allow anyone to abuse her--physically or verbally.

"Cooo, cooo," Songbird lamented as she flew in the sky. It was another cool morning and after another uneventful day trying to find a nesting place, she was wasting no time in trying to find one today. Time was running out. This time, her mate Strongfeather, was flying with her. They agreed that working together they could cover more area before darkness fell. While soaring around, Songbird spotted a nice setting that appeared safe, but it wasn't a tree. It was high enough to protect her eggs from predators and as she flew closer she noticed it was near enough to the ground for her and Strongfeather to be able to search for food. This was the spot! She called for Strongfeather. He flew down to where she was. "Do you think this is okay?" Songbird asked. Strongfeather knew they didn't have a lot of time to look for anything else, so he said, "Yes, let's build it here." "Good. Okay, find some branches to build the nest," Songbird replied. They found an area nearby where branches were covering the ground, so they had no problems quickly building their nest.

It was Sunday and Keisha rushed to church. She needed her spirit rejuvenated and going to church was one of the things that really uplifted her. After singing and crying and saying "Hallelujah," Keisha, left feeling good about herself. She cooked a quick meal for the kids; their favorite – chicken nuggets and fries, and while they were eating she looked in the newspaper for a job. Today she was feeling positive there would be something other than an Engineering job in the classified ads, because she knew that the best jobs would be posted in the Sunday edition. In the background she kept hearing "Cooo, cooo," but didn't pay any attention to it. Since it wasn't too cool outside, Keisha decided to read the paper on the patio while having a cup of coffee.

While sitting on the patio, Keisha noticed a light brown bird with black tipped wings flying close with a small branch between its little black beak. "Where is that bird going with that twig in its mouth?" she thought. It landed softly on her planter. She had seen similar birds feeding off the grounds near her patio, but never paid any attention to them. She sat very quietly just to see what it would do. It laid the branch in her plant. "That's the plant I just transplanted," she murmured. Her first reaction was to shoo the bird away, but for some unknown reason she just sat there. Fascinated, she continued to watch, and soon after, another bird came over. They began to work in concert. The first bird that arrived stood up on the rim of the planter and pulled the twig from the other bird's beak and laid it in the dirt. The second bird would leave and return with another twig and the other bird would take it and place it in the dirt. They did this the entire day until they had a well-covered nest. Keisha was impressed by their collaborative effort and silent ease in which they performed their task. "If only I could find a mate or partner who worked that way, I'd be all right," she humorously thought. "Well, at least someone is able to take care of their home," Keisha said under her breath.

At that moment, the newspaper fell to the floor and snapped her out of her revelry. "I need to find a job instead of worrying about some birds," she thought. So Keisha decided to finish reading her paper inside and figure out what to do with her new visitors later. "I wonder if I can get money for having a bird sanctuary," she mused as she walked inside. That night before she went to bed, Keisha remembered the birds and looked outside to see if they were still there. Sure enough, one was on the plant with its face tucked inside its folded wings. The bird looked so peaceful that Keisha felt bad about sending it away. "I guess they can stay as long as they don't make a mess," she said. Well, looks like it's time for me to go to bed too," she said out loud. So she turned out the lights and did just that.

"Cooo, cooo," sang Songbird. It was morning and time for her to eat. "Cooo, cooo," Strongfeather replied. He was letting Songbird know that he heard her and was on his way. Songbird flew out of the nest and onto the ground to scrounge up worms and anything edible that she could find. She would nibble at the ground and look up for predators in the rhythmic manner she always did. By that time, Strongfeather arrived and they busily gathered food together in the same way. They decided to leave from there because Strongfeather heard of a feeding ground in an area where there was freshly tousled grass and plenty of food for all.

Their earlier cooing woke Keisha, but she didn't mind. It was a comforting sound as opposed to her waking to the sounds of bulldozers and large tractor mowers. Over the last few months the city had been clearing the lot next door where an intermediate school was about to be built. The area was growing fast. Three years ago, she used to see rabbits jumping in front of her patio and cows herding in the field next door. Now all she sees everywhere is land cleared away for apartment complexes, strip malls and banks.

Keisha found a couple of promising jobs in the paper and was eager to start her day early, just like the birds. "They say the early bird catches the worm," Keisha mused aloud. She chuckled to herself at the thought. While having her coffee and a slice of toast on the patio, she noticed the birds were gone so she peeked into the nest. She wondered where the birds were and if they planned to return. As she leaned over to peek into the nest, some crumbs from the toast fell into the nest. God knows I can't feed me and these kids---let alone some birds, she thought. "Oh, what the heck?!" As she said this, Keisha broke off a piece of toast and crumbled it into the nest. Times aren't that bad that I can't share my bread with a bird. She walked back into the apartment. She applied for a few of the jobs online and called a couple of places to schedule an interview. One company asked her a few pre-screening questions and based on her responses asked her to attend a panel interview later that week. "Thank you, God!" Keisha said aloud. She was excited about the possibility and couldn't wait to tell her kids when they came home from school.

By noontime, Songbird knew it was soon time to lay her eggs, so she left Strongfeather at the feeding ground and flew back to the nest. When she settled into the nest, she was surprised to see bread crumbs sprinkled in the dirt. The human must have put it there, she thought. She and Strongfeather had kept an eye on the human while building their nest the previous evening. They were mildly surprised that they were not shooed away. This was interesting because even though she had managed to keep away from them, Songbird knew of fellow doves that weren't so lucky. Humans were typically anything but oblivious to the birds. And as a result, many birds were either run over or killed by the humans' fast moving machines or shot while flying in the air. In spite of this knowledge and her extremely cautious nature, she felt the human who lived on the patio didn't seem quite as dangerous. As a matter of fact, Songbird thought to herself, "she didn't bother us when she saw us building our nest." But her instincts told her they still could not be trusted. Songbird felt some contractions in her belly and knew it was time to lay her eggs. "Cooo, cooo, coo" she cried as one egg and then another dropped softly into the nest. She must have cooed a dozen times from the excitement! They're finally here, she thought. Strongfeather will be so pleased when he sees them. Exhausted from delivering the eggs, Songbird fell asleep.

When the kids came home from school, Keisha excitedly told them about her job interview. The kids noticed a change in their Mom's attitude and were relieved. She seemed to be back to her pleasant self. Even though they didn't tell her, the twins were worried that they may end up being homeless like a friend of theirs whose parents lost their job. That's why they didn't bother her when they needed money for school projects. "Hey, you want to see something really cool?" Keisha asked the kids. "Come this way," she said softly as she motioned them to follow her out to the patio. She opened the blinds and quietly opened the glass door. There lay Songbird asleep in the nest. "That's so cool," Kerri exclaimed. Kyle immediately said, "Mom, that's a dove. We studied about them in science class," he said. "You have a dove in your plant. How did that happen?" Kyle asked. "I'm not sure," Keisha replied. "They showed up yesterday with branches and started building a nest in it. Doves, huh? Well, maybe that's a good sign, you know." "Remember the story about Noah and the Ark?" Keisha asked the kids. "Well, after it rained for 40 days and nights, Noah asked God to give him a sign that there was land somewhere. So, God sent a dove with a twig in its beak as a sign that everything was all right. Maybe this is God's way of telling us everything is going to be all right," Keisha said enthusiastically. "A dove's nest in my plant may be a good thing," Keisha added as she closed the sliding glass door. "Mom, can I feed them?" Kerri asked. "Feed them what?" Keisha asked at first in a bothered tone. "What about some bread or something?" replied Kerri. "I did drop some toasted crumbs in the nest earlier this morning, but I don't know if we should bother them too much. We might frighten them away. If they aren't there later, I'll help you put some in their nest, okay?" Keisha replied. Kerri said, "Cool" as she skipped to her bedroom satisfied with her mother's suggestion. She couldn't wait to tell her friends at school tomorrow.

It was near dusk and Keisha heard the familiar "coo-coo" coming from her patio. She rushed to the sliding door to see what was going on. What she saw next was amazing. Singing all the while, a dove flew up to the top of her patio near the planter. The other dove that was in the nest spread its wings and perched its small legs on the back of the planter; coo-cooed and flew off. At that very moment Keisha saw them---two small eggs lying on the dirt in between the mounds of branches and debris its parents had strategically placed beneath the plant. The other dove softly landed on the edge of the planter and then placed itself gently on the eggs. It folded its wings across each other and covered the eggs completely. Then it tucked its head inside its breast and went to sleep. Keisha also noticed that the crumbs were gone. She debated if she should give them more, but she was cautious. She knew that all animals were very protective of their eggs and didn't want to do anything to upset them.

She walked away trying to figure out a way to give the bird some crumbs, but couldn't come up with anything. She folded some clothes and put them up. She passed the glass door again. "That's it! I'm just going to put a few on the corner of the nest and pray it doesn't peck my eyes," she said. She toasted a slice of bread, crumbled it up and placed it in a storage bag. She gently opened the sliding glass door and slowly pushed the screen open. She moved a chair near the planter and eased one foot at a time on the seat so that she was standing in a safe position where she could safely jump if the dove attacked her. Then she slowly grabbed a hand full of crumbs from the bag and carefully placed them near the very edge inside the planter. The dove didn't move. Keisha quickly moved away and jumped down from the chair feeling relieved she didn't have to fight a dove and elated that it trusted her enough to take her food. She smiled as she walked back into the house.

Three times daily for over two weeks, Strongfeather and Songbird switched places--allowing each one to eat and get something to drink while protecting their babies. They would switch early in the morning, in the afternoon and right before dusk. Their cooing would wake Keisha every morning and she looked forward to seeing their ritual throughout the day. Her kids were even getting involved. They hurried to finish their homework and eat so that they could watch the doves switch places. They would sit patiently inside the sliding glass door and as soon they heard the cooing, they would call out for their mother to signal the beginning of the ritual. Once a week Keisha would let them put crumbs in the nest for the doves. One day they even got a chance to look at the eggs when both of the doves were away. They all peeked into the nest and saw two small eggs about the size of a small child's fist. They were covered in periwinkle blue and speckled brownish-black spots and looked so vulnerable lying among the twigs, branches and ivy leaves. Everyone was filled with anticipation about what they would look like once they hatched.

While the doves were taking care of their unhatched eggs, Keisha was diligently looking for a job. The job interview she had a week ago went very well and she felt confident she would get a call back. The job was something she hadn't done before, but she was very familiar with the company. Even though the company had been around nearly 50 years, it was very liberal and diverse. It didn't hurt either that the company was investing a lot of money into a new project that she would be a part of and if she did well, it would lead to greater opportunities. Keisha was excited. It looked like the doves were definitely a good thing to have around. Since she had a little money left over after paying all of her bills, Keisha went to the store and bought a small bag of birdseed. They'll probably need this when the babies are hatched, she thought as she placed a hand full in the nest. Little did she know it was going to be sooner rather than later.

It was morning and Songbird knew it was about time for her eggs to hatch. They had started moving around inside the egg a couple of days ago and had been increasing in activity ever since. She felt the first one begin breaking out of the shell with its beak. Then the other one came out slowly. "Coo-coo, Coo-coo," she cried out. "Coo-coo, Coo-coo," she repeated. As is tradition in the dove world, a hatched egg is greeted with a lot of cooing. So, Songbird cooed as loudly as she could and as long as her breath would allow. She just knew that Strongfeather would be able to hear her cries and would rush to see the hatchlings, but to no avail. "Coo-coo," she cooed again. Strongfeather didn't respond. She hoped he was okay. "Coo-coo," she cooed again. She needed to make sure they were fed when they woke up, but Strongfeather didn't respond. Luckily, the human had left some food in the nest to eat. She was thankful because she could feed them now instead of having to leave them unattended while she searched for food. She would do this until Strongfeather arrived. She wouldn't allow herself to think anything bad had happened. She just focused on her chicks.

Keisha was making up her bed that morning when she heard loud and numerous cries coming from the patio. She instinctively knew something different was going on with the doves. Normally, each dove would cry out a "coo" and the other would answer before they switched places, but this time it was louder than normal and sounded like one of the doves was in distress. Keisha rushed to the glass window and looked out. She noticed the bird was alone and still cooing. So, she opened the patio door and jumped to stand on the chair. She placed the chair at a safe distance so that she wouldn't frighten the dove but close enough to see what was going on inside the nest. She leaned over and peeked inside. Songbird moved her wing a little bit to show off her babies. She was so proud;

besides she trusted this human, so it was okay. Keisha saw two small, dark brown baby doves barely moving surrounded by broken shell pieces. They were covered in some creamy-looking matter, but Keisha could see they were breathing. "Oh my God, you had babies," Keisha happily announced to Songbird. "They are beautiful," she said tearfully. "I know you're probably hungry, so I'll get you some more bird feed." Keisha ran into the house and got a scoop of bird feed and poured a little bit on the side away from the babies. She was still leery about the mother, especially now that her eggs were hatched. After placing the feed in the nest, Keisha went back inside.

About an hour or so later she heard cooing noises again coming from the patio. She went outside and noticed the other dove had taken the place of the mother dove. By that time, the baby doves were awake and hungry. Keisha watched with adoration as the dove fed its babies. It would lean its head back and push the food it had eaten up through its throat to the edge of its beak and then gently push its beak inside the small beak of the baby dove and push the food down its throat. It did this to each dove until they were full and fell back asleep.

The phone rang and Keisha ran inside to catch it. "Hello, this is Keisha." "Ms. Jackson, this is Vickie Patrick from Doran Corporation. We met when you attended our open house and interviewed with some of our colleagues a couple of weeks ago." "Yes, I remember you," Keisha said evenly (as if that was going to make her heart stop beating so fast). "First, I want to tell you everyone was very impressed with you. After your interview, we had to raise the bar of expectations from the other candidates we interviewed." "Thank you." Keisha responded. "Our main concern is that since your experience is on a senior level and this position is not, what's going to prevent you from leaving if you got an offer more aligned with your background?" After finding her breath, Keisha responded with three key reasons (even though she could have given ten) why she was committed to working with the company if she was hired. She silently prayed that Vickie was comfortable with her responses and would favorably rally her colleagues to offer her the position. Vickie thanked her for her response and told her she would be in contact soon with their decision.

After the call, Keisha felt uneasy and highly emotional. She was alternately laughing and crying. She was happy they were impressed with her, but worried that they wouldn't hire her because they felt she was overqualified and would leave if a better opportunity came along. She really wanted this job! "I've done all that I can do. There is nothing left but to let go and let God. Lord, I'm asking you to intervene on behalf. I can't do this alone. I'm praying that you put me in their favor, Father!"

she cried out loud. Keisha knew that only prayers could ease her troubled heart and she did just that for what seemed like hours before the kids rushed in from school.

Songbird had been with the birds all day and it was beginning to get hard now for her and Strongfeather to keep up with their feedings. The first-born was stronger than the second born. It ate more and chirped the loudest. Songbird made sure she fed the second born, because she knew that with time he would be as strong as his brother. When they got older, she and Strongfeather would name them. For now, they were just concerned with feeding them. Even with the birdseeds, they had to search for food more often. It was almost time for the switch and Strongfeather hadn't called out. "Cooo-cooo," Songbird cried out. "Cooo-cooo," she cried again. "Cooo-cooo," she repeated, but no response. Darkness was falling and still no sight of Strongfeather. Songbird knew something was wrong. She hated to leave her babies, but they were going to be hungry soon and she didn't have enough food for them. Besides, she needed to find out what happened to Strongfeather, so she flew off trusting that the babies would be okay.

It had been a week since the baby doves hatched and they were getting stronger. They were moving around and chirping continuously. Keisha was amazed at how fast they were growing. However, she also noticed that one dove was smaller than the other. The larger one was able to eat faster than the smaller one and, subsequently, ate more food. But the smaller one was a fighter and he would push his beak close to the feeding dove's beak to make sure it got some of the food before the larger one would move him out of the way. Kerri and Kyle were so excited they decided to give them both a name. Kerri wanted to name the smallest one because "he may be small, but he makes sure he eats." She named him Little Beak. Kyle named the bigger one, Big Dove, "because it was the biggest, of course." When Keisha noticed it was close to the time for the doves to switch she looked outside to check on them. She thought she heard cooing earlier, but she was so used to them by now that she didn't pay much attention. That's when she noticed the nest was empty except for the baby doves. She called the kids and they all took turns standing on the chairs to see the little wonders. There they were moving and chirping around in the nest. Keisha wondered where the other doves were. It wasn't their nature to leave their babies unprotected like this— especially after sundown. She feared the worse and hoped for the best, so she decided to stay around until another dove showed up.

Songbird searched in all the familiar places, but she didn't find Strongfeather and it was getting close to the babies' feeding time. She did find Grandmother Dove who was the oldest living dove in their set.

(That's why everyone called her Grandmother Dove). She explained that Strongfeather never appeared for the last feeding of the day and she needed to find food for the babies. Grandmother Dove didn't hesitate to step in and help. Songbird guided her to the nest and then flew off to find food and search for Strongfeather. Grandmother Dove approached the nest and noticed that a human was sitting near the doves. She almost flew away, but she knew she had to protect the babies, so she eased onto the nest and settled over the sleeping baby doves while cautiously keeping an eye on the human. Songbird didn't mention this to her. She had a lot of explaining to do. "Why would she build a nest so close to humans?" she thought. "She knows humans can't be trusted." That's when the human left and Grandmother Dove settled in for a little nap before the hungry babies woke up. Grandmother Dove was awakened by an unfamiliar sound. She didn't move she just opened her eyes. It was the human and she was moving close to the nest with something in her hands. Grandmother Dove became alarmed and was poised to protect and attack. She extended her wings out to each side of her body as wide as they could go and snapped them at the human. The human yelled and immediately jumped back. Grandmother Dove didn't go back to sleep, she was on high alert. "How could Songbird do this to her own babies?" she thought as she watched the human leave the patio.

While sitting on the patio keeping an eye on the baby doves, Keisha noticed a bigger dove fly to the nest and settle in. It was larger with darker brown feathers and wider wings. Even its beak was a little wider than the other ones. Despite the fact that this was a new bird, Keisha still decided to put some seeds in the nest before she went to bed. She went inside and got a cup of seeds and as usual moved her chair near the nest so she wouldn't have to lean too far over without losing her balance. As she leaned forward and reached to pour in the seeds, the bird opened it wings as wide as it could and fiercely snapped her! "Whoa!" Keisha yelled. She almost fell out of chair as she jerked her hand back away from the nest. Keisha rushed inside the house from the patio after her little fiasco with the new dove. Obviously, it's not used to humans. Not like the other doves that seemed to trust her. Keisha told the kids about it and they started laughing when she said told them she almost fell when the dove snapped her with its strong wings. "It stung a little, but scared me a lot because she attacked me by surprise. If she weren't protecting the baby doves, we'd be having dove for dinner tomorrow!" Keisha said jokingly. "I didn't know their wings were so strong," she laughed while shaking her head as she left the kids room. She'll never try to feed *Big Bertha* again and that's for sure!

After a long time of searching, Songbird finally found Strongfeather. He had located a new feeding ground that was far from their nest. However, by the time he got to the new ground, he realized it was time to switch with Songbird. But since Songbird didn't have enough food to feed the baby doves, he decided to stay anyway and try and get more food. Songbird was relieved to have found him. She told him to return to the nest and let her feed for a while. Strongfeather returned home and found Grandmother Dove minding the chicks. He greeted her and they switched places. After telling her where to find Songbird, Grandmother met up with her and they decided to go to another nesting area. "Why didn't you tell me about the human, Songbird?" asked Grandmother Dove. "She tried to attack the babies last night. How could you be so careless? You know humans can't be trusted." Songbird tried to explain, but Grandmother Dove kept on. Finally, Songbird was able to get a word in and that's when she told Grandmother Dove of her dilemma of not having a nesting place to lay her eggs and how she later found the perfect spot to build the nest---not realizing it was part of the human's home. "Surprisingly, she never did anything to us; she just fed us bird seed. She was probably trying to feed you," cooed Songbird. "The human never bothers us and she's very quiet." "Well, she probably won't be feeding you anytime soon after what I did," exclaimed Grandmother Dove. She explained to Songbird how she snapped at the human when she moved close to the planter and Songbird shook her head in dismay. "How could you Grandmother Dove?" Songbird asked. "My first charge was to protect those babies and that's what I was doing," Songbird knew how Grandmother Dove felt about humans and she also knew they were going to need her to help feed the babies, so she said nothing further. They were both tired from their busy night, so they fell asleep for a quick nap.

The next day Keisha was anxious to phone in her unemployment claim. She still had not heard back from the Doran Corporation, but the rent was due and with the remaining money in her savings account and her unemployment check, she would just be able to pay it with little left for anything else. Despite the gloomy situation, Keisha was feeling good about everything. She had managed to pay her rent through the worst of times and not one light flickered. She felt that if the doves could make it despite everything that they have to go through to survive; she was going to make it too. Unfortunately, this enthusiasm wouldn't last long. When Keisha had finished answering the questions on the phone to file her unemployment claim, the automatic voice recording told her that her last payment was received two weeks ago. Keisha's heart fell to the ground. She ran into the bedroom to find her last unemployment check stub and there written in small letters at the bottom of her check—"***last*** *payment*." She immediately called the unemployment office and inquired about an extension and was told that Congress hadn't passed legislation to extend unemployment benefits for the State of Texas. She was devastated! She cried out, "God help me, I can't do anything else! I surrender my all to you because only you can help me through this!" As she cried, she remembered the gospel song, His Eye Is on the Sparrow by Civilla Martin, they used to sing in the church when she was a little girl, "*Why should I feel discouraged / Why should the shadows come / Why should my heart feel lonely / And long for heaven and home / When Jesus is my portion / A constant friend is He / His eye is on the sparrow / And I know He watches over me...*" That song filled her heart with hope as she looked out the window and saw the baby doves in the nest being fed, but tears flowed from her eyes as she contemplated her situation. During times like these, Keisha wished her grandmother was still alive. She always had an encouraging word whenever Keisha was feeling at her lowest. Just the thought of her Grandmother not being there made her cry even harder. After she composed herself, Keisha called her best friend and told her what happened. Her friend suggested she have a yard sale and use the money to pay her rent. Keisha thought about it and figured why not. Besides, her lease was up that month and she would be free and clear to move in with her mother until she was able to get another job. She didn't want to leave without paying rent because she didn't need to have anything else negative on her credit report. Lord only knows how low her score was since she lost her job and started falling behind on her bills! She had worked hard to clear up her credit before she lost her job, because she was getting ready to buy a house. Now she was going to have start all over.

Big Dove and Little Beak were getting stronger and flapping around more and more in their nest. Songbird, Strongfeather and Grandmother Dove were kept busy trying to keep up with the young doves' increased appetites and had to eat more food to be able to feed them. This meant they were spending more time away from the nest, but they knew the little ones would be fine until they returned. The humans were no problem and the nest was concealed underneath the plant so it would be hard for a predator to find them. One day while they were gone, Big Dove started flapping his wings harder and harder. Little Beak followed. Every time Big Dove would flap his wings, Little Beak would attempt to do the same. Finally, Big Dove flapped its wings hard enough and jumped from the dirt in the planter to its edge. Little Beak did the same thing, but wobbled a little as it perched on the edge. Keisha and the kids watched from inside the glass door in amazement. It was like watching a baby walk for the first time. Too bad she didn't have a camera, Keisha thought. This would be a great video for *America's Funniest Home Videos*. They were always airing videos with animals in them. Since she didn't have one, she and the kids would just have to be content with the memory. After flapping his wings profusely, Big Dove landed on Keisha's barbecue grill. After a couple of attempts, Little Beak landed on the top of the grill following Big Dove. Big Dove was feeling brave and free and he wanted to try to fly further. He flapped his wings a bit more and was able to successful fly from the grill onto the top of the patio rail. It took Little Beak several unsuccessful attempts, but he was able to do the same. Then after a couple of flaps, Big Dove flew to the ground.

The baby doves didn't notice him, but Strongfeather was returning to the nest to feed them when he saw them fly to the edge of the planter. He didn't want to stop their progress, because he knew it was time for them to leave the nest, but he wanted to be there for them in case they weren't totally ready, so he watched from a small tree near the patio. Little Beak wasn't as strong as Big Dove, but he had determination! Every little flight Big Dove made, Little Beak would follow or at least try. They were flapping around on the ground and finally Big Dove started flying back and forth from the ground to the patio rail. Unfortunately, Little Beak wasn't as strong and couldn't fly as far as his brother yet, so Strongfeather flew down to make sure he was okay. Finally, after flapping for a little while back and forth, Big Dove flew near Strongfeather and they flew away. Unfortunately, Little Beak couldn't make it, so he stayed on the ground underneath a hedge that was planted by Keisha's bedroom window. Strongfeather showed Big Dove where their set was living and everyone greeted him with admiration at how fast he learned how to fly. Shortly after he left, Strongfeather returned to check on Little Beak who was still having problems flying off the ground. For the remainder of the day, Strongfeather taught Little Beak how to find food and protect himself while feeding. In between feeding lessons, Little Beak was still flapping his wings as fast as his body allowed. He was determined to fly away like Big Dove, so he kept trying and trying.

Songbird flew back to the nest and saw Strongfeather and Little Beak feeding from the ground. "Hi, little one," she said. "I'm so proud of you." Little Beak flapped his wings to show his Mom that he could fly. He pounced up on the hedge branch and because he was flapping so hard, he started to fly higher and higher. Before he knew it, he was flying higher than the patio ledge and into a small tree nearby. They all flew away and met up with Big Dove and the other mourning doves. As Songbird sat on the tree branch admiring her doves flying from one tree to another, she thought of the human who had treated them so kindly. Without her help, the babies would not have been able to survive. She gained a new respect for humans. She remained cautious of them, but she knew that there were some humans who treated animals kindly and she had met one.

While the kids watched the doves fly away, Keisha went back into the bedroom to put the final stickers on the items she was planning to sell. She decided to have an estate sale instead of a yard sale this way people could walk through her apartment and carry out anything they wanted. Anything left over would be packed and stored. Kerri rushed into the room. "Mom, Big Dove and Little Beak are gone," she said sadly. "Well, sweetie that's what they do," explained Keisha. "Birds don't stay in the nest for long. Look how fast they grew up. They were laid in a day and hatched in a couple of weeks and were flapping around soon thereafter. They aren't like humans who take a long time to leave home." "Yeah, but I miss them," said Kerri. Not as much as I will, Keisha said to herself. Keisha thought about the peace she felt when she was watching the whole process--from the first time she saw the doves to the baby doves hatching. If nothing else, they left her with a renewed awareness of how nature is connected to everything from the earth to the birds and everything in between. She gained a new respect for life itself and confidence that despite whatever a person is going through, life still goes on. She also discovered that when people face adversities in life they need to know that everything will be all right. It could be an encouraging word from someone, a smile or just to hear how someone else with a similar problem was able to work through it.

While Keisha was in the kitchen, Kerrin and Kyle called for her. "Mom, come see what we've done to help you." That could only mean one thing--more work for her, so Keisha ran to go see what damage they caused all the while hoping it was minimal. Imagine her surprise when she went into the room. They had laid out all of their toys, video games and board games for the estate sale. Kerrin even put out all of her favorite dolls. "Mom we want to sell our things to help you get money for rent. We can always get more for Christmas, but we know you need the help," they said together. Tears welled up in Keisha's eyes at the kind and unselfish act of her kids. "Thank you my babies," she said as she hugged each one tightly.

Keisha was able to sell a lot of items at the estate sale and pay her rent. Even though she didn't have a lot of money left over and she still did not have a job, Keisha knew that everything was going to be okay. As she cleaned up her empty apartment, Keisha noticed the planter hanging on her patio and thought of her experience with the doves. "God, thank you for sending them to me," she said. She wasn't quite sure if they were sent to her as a sign that everything would be okay, but they did help her to see things in a positive manner. Their tenacity and courageousness in the face of adversity mirrored her own life at that time. So it was in that same way, the doves had helped ease her troubled heart and recognize that she too could find the strength to move on.

The patio was the last area Keisha cleaned, but she left the planter with the remnants of the dove's nest still in it for the new tenants. "Who knows?" she thought. They may need a dove in the nest.

Life Is Good To Me Because I Am Good To Life

By Lynn Simpson, MBA

I say this because despite all of the ups and downs in this life of mine I have grown

I say this because through all of my trials and tribulations I have grown

I say this because though my times of weakness and defeat I have grown

I say this because even when I thought this trial time wasn't going to pass, it did and I grew

I have grown because I have learned that through it all the life I have is the life I have created for myself and here I am

Life is good to me because I am good to Life!

My life is perfect because I make it a perfect day everyday, even on THOSE days…

My life has evolved in many ways, I have grown

My life is my life and I wouldn't change one day, one minute or one second of it

It is my life

Life is good to me because I am good to Life!

I could have taken many different paths and thrown in the towel many years ago, but I didn't because my life lessons have made me who I am

I stand here today because of my goodness and faith in life!

Life is good to me because I am good to Life!

Manual NOT Included

By Lynn Simpson, MBA

When sitting on the sideline observing, the task looks so easy, in your mind you are saying, "How hard can that be?" As you look on in amazement, your mind is calculating all of the necessary steps to complete the task. For example, when watching a contortionist as they twist and turn their bodies with amazing movements, your mind is thinking, I can do that! Then you attempt the movements, you stretch and prepare your body for the actions you just witnessed and quickly realize the movements are out of your scope of immediate achievement but with practice, it can happen. To look at the activity, it looked so easy until you tried it for yourself, and realized it only *appears* to be easy. That is the same way parenting can be. We have witnessed so many people parent and from the sidelines it appears to come so easily, that is, until you are the person who is *actually* doing the parenting.

I've been a parent for more than half of my life, and although it looks like an easy job it isn't. Being a parent has been the most challenging job that I have done. The job of a parent isn't one that you can walk away from because you no longer want to be a parent. The hours are long and the pay, *wait*... there isn't a salary for this job, but it requires all that you have to be successful! Raising a child requires a great deal of patience, nurturance, and more love than you ever thought possible.

I was a young mother with the odds against me. You know, the young, single parent with the full life options appearing to disappear right before your eyes because you did the unthinkable... getting pregnant *before* putting your dreams in motion. I learned along the way that it isn't so much about the getting pregnant at a young age, as it is about not having a dream before doing so.

Not having a dream is what creates the long treacherous road that lies before many young parents. I was always a dreamer. I have dreamt from childhood that I would be something special in my life. While I was never really sure what that something was, I just knew deep within that it was something special and that I MUST keep working towards it!

I remember the day I realized a new life was coming into the world. Being surprised is an understatement! I had dreams of going to New York City to the Fashion Institute of Technology. The day I learned about the bundle of joy that was about to enter the world, my first question to anyone that could hear me was, "Does this mean I'm not going away to school?" Although no one answered the question, I knew I had to ditch those plans since having a baby at college wasn't really an option. I had to come up with another plan quickly! It's amazing how one day the world is your oyster and the next you are setting up a crib.

For me, I am one of the lucky ones. I had dreams and I held onto them, although they were tucked away for the time. While many were going off to college after high school graduation, I was going off to work because my responsibilities had changed. Being a young single parent isn't a job I would recommend to anyone.

Let me make this clear - being a single parent isn't solitary just because you aren't married. Oh no, it's single in every sense of the word. You are responsible for *everything* that the child will need from financial support, midnight feeding, sleepless nights, and there are many of those. I am so fortunate that I had my mother, sister and grandmother to help me along the way. While I knew that my life as a single young woman had changed the day my child was born, I was ok with the decisions that I made for us.

I remember asking God, "Please guide me" because I didn't have a clue what parenting entailed. And I promised that I would do whatever it took to make her the best person that I could. Yes, I made mistakes, heck they didn't even send me home with a manual, only a brand new life. Well, let's see, you want me to get up in the middle of the night and do what? I'm sleepy and I need my rest. I didn't know I signed up for this. I had to *quickly* get into the swing of getting up in the middle of the night to tend to my child.

Let's remember I was still attending high school waiting for my graduation. *Luckily for me, I had spent my summers during high school taking classes for early graduate, however, when the time came, I decided not to follow through with early graduation, and so I didn't have many classes to complete.* When the middle of the night feedings would come, which they seemed to come quite frequently, I would often ask the question, "Didn't she just eat?" Not that the question made a difference to the infant that was longing for her bottle. I had to learn quickly that my schedule no longer belonged to me. Like it or not! Thank God for my sister because *lawd* knows if it wasn't for her, a midnight feeding wasn't going to happen in a timely manner. I mean, really, didn't she just eat like two hours ago? This is an example of not being ready for what was to come. During this time I learned quickly and saw the importance of planning and taking the advice from those that had walked a mile in what was now my new experience.

I learned that being a single parent is a full-time job with a great deal of overtime.

Being a role model was important to me. I always raised the bar higher and higher. When I wanted to set an example, I would do it first. It bothers me when I hear adults ask children after high school graduation, "What are you going to do now?" Shouldn't the question be "What school are you planning on attending?"

I know school isn't for everyone, yes, I have heard that a million times and maybe it isn't, however, removing it as an option seems to give free rein to lack mobility, plans or dreams. I know education isn't always the ticket to all of life's dreams, however it can certainly open a few more doors. In my house, the first four years of college were mandatory! No questions asked. I made that point very clear during the elementary school days. I would ask the question, "What would you like to go to college to study?" I realized she may not have understood the question completely at the time, but I knew if I asked her enough she would have a clear answer by the time she was ready to really make the decision. I didn't wait until the last minute to plant those seeds; I started very early and made sure it was ingrained in her mind.

For me, I began by attending the community college and then I transferred to a four-year university. I was determined to complete my educational goals before my daughter went off to college herself. Obtaining my college degree was a dream of mine, although it took me a long time to complete the task for many reasons, but I did it. I accomplished my mission one month before my daughter graduated from high school. May 2002, *I* walked the stage at Rider University graduating with a double major. You talk about full circle - at my high school graduation I was a mother to a six-week old and now here she is at my college graduation, eighteen years later. Wow, what a great day! I have always vowed that *I* would be a role model and not leave that responsibility to any strangers. I was blessed to have been surrounded with people who would serve as mentors and educators to help me mold and guide the progression of her life. That was very important to me.

I knew I couldn't do it all because I didn't know it all, but there were people out there who could offer the things I didn't know. At the age of eight she was "working" at Nu Vou on Saturdays, where she learned how to run a business. *Yes, she was only eight years old. She was an advanced child; just to give you an idea, she began walking at nine months old.* And from that experience she had her own vendor business called "Jingles". Her mentor Kim would take her to New York City so she could purchase her goods to sell at the events they would attend. I kept her away from those that didn't represent growth and understood she would meet that group, as she got older. Let's face it the world consists of many and our paths will eventually cross, however, when you have a strong foundation those groups only serve as a reminder of what not to do.

When I was planning out our lives, there were a few things that were important to me and the success of my child. Education was at the top of the list. My family and I made sure the best educational foundation was set. The Simpson trio didn't spare any expenses when it came to our child. So off to school she went. The school was just around the corner from our home and the education was great quality. That's what was very important.

During the private school days, I gave up a few things just to make sure the tuition was paid to ensure her continued enrollment. There were times when I worked several jobs just to make sure we had what we needed. After all she was *MY* responsibility and mine alone as it turned out. I took my job as a parent serious, and it didn't matter what I had to do to get the job done. Again and again, I thank God for my mother, sister and grandmother because without them I don't know what I would have done. What a blessing to have had four mothers, all of which offered a different set of values in her life.

Transitioning

There was a time in the early years that I thought about setting up a parent abuse hotline. Here's why: At 9:00 p.m. *EVERY* night for over a year we would go through a process because it was bedtime. I made sure I went through the entire steps to ensure a smooth transition.

We would begin at 8:00 p.m. with our nightly routine; bath, lotion, massage, *check*; snack, *check*; read a story, *check*; pray, *check*; kisses, *check*. Ok, we are on schedule at 8:59 p.m. "Good night Love Angel" in the sweetest voice I could muster up because I knew what was to come. I was praying, maybe this would be the night that she cooperated. And then it would happen. The screaming at the top of her lungs about how she wasn't sleepy and not ready to go to bed. "GRANDMA, I'm hungry! I need something to drink. Grandmaaaa!!!!! I'm serious, this is ridiculous, I'm starving!" All this coming from a four year old, *lawd* give me strength! *I never understood why she wasn't sleepy because I certainly was!* Not only did she refuse to go to sleep, when her screaming didn't prove to be effective, she would also sneak and call our Aunt Berniece and tell her about what we were putting *her* through since she wasn't ready for bed. I'll tell you, I had my hands full. In turn our Dear Aunt Bern, would then call us back and strongly suggest that we give her what she wants as she laughs about what *we* were going through. "Are you kidding, she called *you*? She has had her snack already. This is just her plot to drive me insane!" Why me? Our neighbors would know what time it was without looking at a clock after sundown based on the crying. I would often ask God, why on earth are you putting me through this? I couldn't understand what lesson I was supposed to get from this *nightly* horror of an experience.

But then I realized it was a part of the job. Mom said, "It would be days like this!" This is when I came up with this great idea. *All parents who suffer from bedtime blues should come together and create a parent abuse hotline.* Of course it didn't happen, but just thinking about it made the process so much easier. My lesson from my bedtime nightmare was *learning to ignore things that I couldn't change, and change the things that I can.* It was during these times I learned the Serenity Prayer. God did answer my prayer. She eventually stopped crying at bedtime, but what I didn't mention was that it was more than a year later. God has a way of getting your attention, that's for sure!

Being a parent allowed me to venture into areas that I might otherwise not have and my bedtime experience certainly paved the way. For example learning the serenity prayer, reading self-help books and studying meditation and prayer to get you through the trying times when all you have is time and the ear of God.

As I mentioned before and I will say it again, I **do not** recommend parenting to young women. It is a job that requires far more than you are equipped with at a young age. Trust me on that one! Your biological clock isn't running out. If God has intentions on you having children, you will have them. Take this time out for yourself and live it fully. Write down your dreams and create a path that will allow you to live them. I am grateful for my experience and I wouldn't change one thing, not one thing! It is because of my experiences that have made me who I am today! I have learned and have grown so much. Until this day I still call her my *Love Angel.* I came to realize that perhaps I wasn't ready for NYC and the things that living in a big city entailed. Let's face it; I was very young and not ready for the big streets of New York. Well, that's how I look at. Everything happens just as it should. Our lessons are to be learned and we should grow from them.

During this time of learning and growing, God took my sister home with him since her work here on earth was completed. I am ever so thankful to have had her as my co-parent because without her I don't know what I would have done. During this time I really learned what it was to be a single parent since she was a great deal of help to me. She was an inspiration to my whole family. Karen was the person who would do whatever she could to make sure we were all taken care of, especially

Shakyra. We miss her dearly and though it's been fifteen years, you can't forget someone that meant so much to you! Her footprints are forever on our hearts.

I realize my life isn't much different than many women out there, who are doing all of the things that I have talked about. I am grateful to be here, in this very place and still looking forward to what's to come and leaving behind what isn't. I have learned that because of my role as a mother I was able to take on a different way of thinking and living. Because I was a *single mother*, I began to look for resources that would help me become the best mother possible. We all learn from those around us, but I wanted to learn more. At a very early age I began reading books from the self-help section of the bookstore. I found the reading so fascinating.

The books were talking about me being a better me. Wow I loved it! The more I read, the more I learned. I began to meet people who understood "self-help". They were different; their mindsets were on a different level. This was exactly what I was looking for! It wasn't just about getting through the day and making due with what you have. They were living the lives they had created for themselves; talking to God in a way I have never witnessed before. I remember reading my first book by Ilayna Vanzant. I read this work in 1993, "*Tapping the Power Within*". Boy, talk about opening a new chapter in my world. My mind had been intrigued and from there I learned how to create the life that I wanted for my family and myself.

My very dear friend had gone to a weekend workshop in Maryland called *Life Springs*. When she returned I could immediately see a change in her. It seemed as if she had seen God in the flesh. She had this aura of being free and I knew I wanted that for myself. I told her I wanted to attend the workshop also! *I wanted a piece of the peace that she had experienced!* I wasn't financially able, but I knew this workshop was something I really needed. Being the person that she is, she gifted me the weekend workshop for my birthday! Oh my goodness, I was so excited!

I could hardly wait for the weekend to come. We packed our bags; me, my daughter and the cat Precious and off to Maryland we went. I am still receiving the benefits from that present now more than twelve years later. Since I had already begun my quest for the best life ever, the workshop offered me the opportunity to further my life's journey. Reading and learning all that I could on making the best life that I could was all that I could do. My reading and workshops were all designed to help me be the best parent possible. I was learning the "secret" before the "Secret" was published and didn't even realize it. It's funny how the things we learn are not really understood until they are needed.

I realized early that being an example meant I had to forego many things that might prove unbeneficial to raising a child. It's all a part of the sacrifice, and certainly well worth the efforts. In the process, I learned people will come and go in our lives. People are like seasons in our lives. They will come and they will go. It's just important that we get the lessons from their presence and realize that when the season has ended, the lesson has been completed. They come for reasons, seasons, and for some they stay around for a lifetime. When the season has passed, I allow it to go. As quoted by Deepak Chopra, *"Whatever relationships you have attracted in your life at this moment, are precisely the ones you need in your life at this moment. There is a hidden meaning behind all events, and the hidden meaning is serving your own evolution"*. I learned some time ago when it's time to go, it's time to go.

Learning all of these things has helped me tremendously in all areas of my life, and especially that of being a parent. I have been able to teach these very important things to my daughter. Of course, she didn't always understand the points I was trying to make but now that she is an adult she gets it. I get great joy from seeing her maneuver through this life with the lessons I have taught her, and the older she gets I am certain she will understand even more.

I have found that my best lessons have come from understanding and listening. I am always in the mindset of a student. I learn more from observation and listening than I do by speaking. While we are sent to this world to take on many different quests, a manual is not included. It is our responsibility to find the manual that is best suited for each of us. For me, it's clearly learning to understand myself. I have the need to know and then apply what I have learned. Yes, I believe in karma, and put out only the things in this life that will bear the sweetest fruits for harvest, with the understanding that sometimes the fruit of our labor my produce some sour fruits. That is to be expected. We go through this life on the course of peaks and valleys, which allows us to grow into the people we are today, ever changing, learning, and growing. The process is called living.

Time for Change

I promised myself that I would do the best possible job as a parent and give *all* that was needed for my child to be the best she can be in this world, including my time. I saw her through college, and then I knew it was my time to do something for *myself*. I put the sails to the wind, packed my boxes and I did the thing I had so badly wanted to do for 25 years. I left my home state of New Jersey. I had wanted to leave for a very long time, but realized that with raising a child it was best I stayed close to family and give my daughter the most stable environment possible. But once the mission was accomplished and she graduated college on her birthday, I knew my days in New Jersey were limited.

I managed to stay in New Jersey an entire eight months after her graduation. I had actually been hatching the plan for two years before. As circumstance would have it, when the time was right, it all fell into place and before I knew it, I was on the road heading to my home. I have to admit; it all happened so fast, as I was driving there, I was saying to myself am I really doing this? It was one of the moments I had dreamt of for so long and here it was, it was really happening! I felt like Miss Celie from The Color Purple "I am HERE!" Just me and Cinnamon, the dog, (don't tell her I called her a dog she wouldn't like that.) heading off to a place where we knew no one. I did know a few people about an hour away and that was good for the 'just in cases', but it was my mission to figure it out on my own. And I did!

I would find myself while walking or driving saying aloud, "I did it!" It was such a great feeling, a feeling of accomplishment! I am here and delighted in the decisions that I have made. I put all of my faith in God and allowed it to be as it was designed to be. I will admit I have recruited my family members and friends to come out here with me, and after some "suggestions", my daughter made the transition as well. Yay! I am so happy to have her here with me! Now I have a few more people on the recruitment list I'm working on. I know the move was the best for me and I pray it will be the best for all who venture out of their box and do something they thought impossible. I did it; I did it alone, by myself just as my mother had just five years before me.

A great deal of my strength comes from my mother, who five years ago decided to sell her house and relocate, and she too, did it alone. I can't go wrong coming from a woman with such strength. It is because of her I had the idea to pursue my dreams and never give up on anything that I wanted. I watched my mother raise my sister and I after my father passed away. She purchased a home from her own hard work. She wasn't left a home; she purchased it on her own! I am so proud to have witnessed that accomplishment. Back in those days, women weren't purchasing homes *and* surviving on their own. But my mother has, until this day, still is holding her own and I am so very proud of her! She is my role model! Just the same way I wanted to be my daughter's role model, my mother was mine. Despite all of the peaks and valleys, twist and turns we are here living and breathing all of life's beauty.

I am very happy to say that I raised my daughter to be the absolute best that she can be and settle for nothing less than greatness. When she was attending Rowan University, I realized that if I wanted her to continue with her education I would show her how it's done. I enrolled myself into a graduate program. When I approached her about continuing her education, I was able to say it can be done, and I've done it. I completed my master's degree in August 2005, which was a great achievement, but my reasons for doing so far exceeded the degree. I am an example of what can be done when you put your mind to anything.

Often I would tell her when she completed graduate school, we would each enroll in a Doctorate program and become doctors together. She completed her master's degree December 2009, I am so very proud of her. So, I guess that means we are going to be doctors! We have gone through our lives together and have grown in ways that seemed impossible. We are still striving to reach all of our goals but just knowing that they are all possible gives us all the strength to continue.

NEVER GIVE UP YOUR DREAMS. All things are possible when you work towards them each and every day. The Simpson's are living proof that it can be done!

But... a Manual is NOT included; you have to create your own.

The Adventures of Isabelle Book I: The Embryo Goddess and the Morpho

By R. Nicole Cutts, PhD

Once upon a time, not so long ago, there was a little goddess in embryo. Her immortal soul had been floating around in the cosmos when, at the moment of her conception, it had been snatched out of the universal atmosphere and brought to earth. She was to be born to mortal parents. Her father, Vata Helios, The Sun Prince, was a magnanimous man who shone like the sun. Her mother, Cythona, The Ice Queen was a beautiful and imperious woman. They both loved each other very much but their coupling was a strange one and at that moment when they came together the planets had been out of their usual alignment. Thus elements of both her mortal parents were in her but there had also been trapped some other material, the origins of which no one knew.

When on the other side, she had asked to come to earth under these exact circumstances to further her soul's education but as soon as she was born and felt the air around her she felt that she had been duped. Before coming to this side she knew that she was a goddess but soon after the moment of birth the forgetting began. Thus she began to feel as if she had been trapped.

"This," the baby goddess, who they named Isabelle, thought, "is NOT what I had in mind."

She shouted to be let out, to go back to whence she came. Her first night on this strange cold planet she screamed the entire time, but no one could understand her. Her piercing cries rang throughout the palace warning all its inhabitants of things to come. (That is why human babies cannot speak. They have just come from the other side and possess all the intelligence of the cosmos. The others, having been here some time, have forgotten most, if not all of it, and do not want to be reminded that they now live in a universe of limited possibility. It is just too much for most mortals to stand really.)

The princess looked like a normal enough beautiful baby human save for a few oddities here and there. She was a sort of reddish brown and had curly brown hair dusted with gold. Like her father, the Sun Prince, she had eyes the color of late summer.

As she grew she became accustomed to this world and started to delight in the odd things she found here; rocks, water, trees, flowers, animals, insects; especially those pretty flying flowers called butterflies. A special few of the other human beings were also very dear to her. She was drawn to anything that sparkled, especially the glint in her father's eyes. She recognized him from the other side and read in his smile a knowing of her too. She was sure it was him because of the one fleck of orange in his right eye.

Her mother, the queen, however beautiful and clever, was foreign and frightening to her. The goddess, now fully thinking of herself as one of them, tried to placate the queen with gifts of flowers and rocks and such; things she herself valued. She loved to play in the forest and during her adventures there would pick the prettiest little flowers to bundle up and tie with blades of grass. She was especially fond of the deep amethyst of the Dog-Tooth violets in the spring. These little offerings she would take and lay at the feet of the queen hoping to win her favor. Momentarily the queen would smile on her but this never lasted for long. The queen was given to fits of rage and anger and during her episodes she would sweep away anything that lay before her, whether it be bunches of flowers or her child.

The goddess, now a little girl, eventually had to give up placating the queen. She could never get it right anyway, could not be what the queen demanded. The girl, never having really let go her true origins, was somehow wild. Like Artemis, she was most content when running wild in the forests and creeks of the kingdom; her pack of dogs, led by her favorite hound; Xerxes, following at her heels. She was often discovered on the hunt dressed in men's clothing, dirty hands and face, hair unkempt. She loved to ride her horses, especially her fastest, Philippides, a jet black Godolohin Arabian that stood sixteen hands, given to her by her father. She sometimes shamelessly rode bare backed into the lake.

The queen tried everything she knew to try and tame her daughter, to turn her into a lady, someone who would be acceptable, who could attract her own wealthy prince one day. If the girl wanted to ride her horses or hunt with bow and arrow, the queen would suggest that she take up some other pursuits. Perhaps cooking, needlepoint or tapestry? When the girl played rough-and-tumble laughing (too loudly) with the other children in the palace, the queen would admonish her. The girl would look at her puzzled, not really hearing much but the phrases "not lady-like" and "unbecoming a princess" were constant refrains. Even her father, who was amused by his spirited daughter, would attempt to domesticate her, discouraging her wild temper often reminding her to be "a nice girl".

At night, safely alone in her chambers the princess tried on the trappings of "a lady". She would bath herself in scented water, oil her skin, and fix her usually unruly hair in some neat style, put on a beautiful gown and sit quietly reading, writing or painting. She secretly delighted in this time. It was often during these sacred times that she would visit the gift her parents had received for her at her birth...

On the day that the queen had learned that she was pregnant with the princess a strange woman dressed in white had appeared at the palace gates. She had come at dawn out of the fog on an unusually cold, late summer morning. This woman had clearly come a long way from the look of her shoes and clothing but she did not look tired, the palace guard noted with curiosity. Neither had his dogs barked, as they usually did, when strangers approached. He asked her to state her business. She told him that she had come on a mission from a far off kingdom and must see the queen and her prince. The guard sent a messenger to the palace and was surprised when word came back that the queen would see the woman. The woman was ushered into the room reserved for audiences with the royal couple.

The prince and his queen sat regally in their respective thrones and waited for her to state her business. Refusing food and water she simply bowed before them and began. "I have come to bring you something that belongs to the daughter you are to bear in the spring." The queen was shocked. How did this strange woman know that she was pregnant? No one had been told, save for the prince. She held her tongue and let the woman continue. It was at this time that the woman drew back her cape to reveal a most resplendent box. This box was the most unusual thing the queen had ever seen and yet it was somehow familiar. Oddly, the prince seemed undisturbed by any of this as he sat quietly smiling at the woman. She stepped forward and placed the box in the queen's hands. The box, which was heavy and encrusted with all manner of gemstones, seemed to give off its own light. On the lid there was embossed an iridescent blue butterfly. The queen, an expert zoologist, who dabbled in entomology, recognized it as the Blue Morpho (M. menelaus). She had been fascinated by this creature in her studies and instantly recalled what she had read.

Surprisingly, the almost metallic blue color of the Morpho is not a result of pigmentation, the wings actually being clear, but is in fact a prime example of iridescence. The microscopic scales covering the Morpho's wings repeatedly reflect incident light at successive layers, leading to interference effects which depend on angle of observance as well as light wavelength. This is why the colors of their wings vary with viewing angle. Although typically forest dwellers, Morphos do make forays into sunny clearings to warm their wings. With the exclusion of mating season, these butterflies typically live alone. The territorial male of the species will chase away any rivals.

Once exploited by the people along the Rio Negro in Brazil, the collected wings of the Blue Morpho were used for adorning ceremonial masks. Aside from humans, the Morpho has few predators. These creatures are poisonous due to the sequestering of poisonous compounds by the feeding caterpillar. From egg to death, the entire life cycle of the Blue Morpho is approximately 115 days. When this butterfly breaks free from its chrysalis, it will have less than a month to live. The woman spoke again. "You are being entrusted with this gift for your child. You must keep it in your possession at all times but you may never open it. Only she may do this at the time and place that she determines. It will be up to you to decide when to give it to her but be clear that it belongs to her."

The queen became indignant. Who was this common woman to tell her what to do with a gift for her child? She spoke up. "I trust you realize to whom you are speaking? Why should we take this gift from you and not look inside the box? How do we know you have not been sent to harm us? We do not even know from what foreign land you have come. How dare you speak to us like this? We do not want your gift and will not accept it! Get out!"

At this the woman rose gently to her full height. She seemed to grow a few inches before she spoke. In a low and even tone, she simply said, "This gift is not for you. It is neither for you to accept or reject. It belongs to the princess and she will have it whether you give it to her or not."

The queen fairly glared at the woman and was about to speak when the prince laid his hand firmly on hers where it gripped her throne. He rose and spoke in a clear strong voice. "Thank you for coming all this way to bring this gift for our child. Her mother and I accept it graciously and will do as you have asked."

The woman smiled looking into his eyes that glinted like sunlight off a forest pool. She brought her hands together as if in prayer and bowed, first to him and then the queen before turning and taking her leave. The prince took the box and left the chamber. The queen was furious at having been crossed and did not speak to the prince for a full month after that.

The prince carried the box down the hallway to his private chamber. He had a special hidden alcove there in the wall. He drew back a heavy velvet curtain the color of amethyst, opened the doors of this sort of tabernacle and placed the box inside. For just a moment he was overwhelmed by emotion and a powerful urge to open the box but he did not dare. His mind flashed forward to the future when he would bestow it upon his daughter, but for now he was content to keep it safely here for her. He closed the door and pulled the heavy curtain back over the space in the wall and returned to his duties.

Sometimes toward the end of her secret nighttime sessions the princess would steal down the long stone hallways to her father's private chamber. After quietly closing the door she would approach the far wall and draw back the heavy amethyst curtain before opening the small door to reveal her gift that lay in wait for her. She always delighted in the light that bounced around in the small space. She ran her hands gently and lovingly over the cool jeweled surface tracing around the butterfly with her finger. Then she would take a deep breath, steadying herself, before opening the box.

Oh, she never opened it more than a crack. Even if she wanted to open it all the way and look inside to see its contents she could not. A brilliant blinding light would escape the tiny crack in the box and she would become overwhelmed by a power that threatened to engulf her. The feeling was indescribable but it mixed the threat of annihilation with such extreme pleasure and potency, the likes of which one could not imagine. She would approach the edge of madness before slamming the box closed again. Panting hard, sometimes sweating, it would take her a moment to collect herself before drawing back her hands. She always concluded this ritual by running her hands over the Morpho once more before bringing her fingers to her lips to kiss them and then places this kiss on the butterfly. After bringing her hands gently to her heart in prayer she would reverse her actions, finally drawing the curtain back over the wall and quietly returning to her bedchamber. Once safely back in her room she undressed and lay on her bed before drifting off into the wildest dreams imaginable.

When the little girl became a young girl her relationship with the queen worsened. Boys, no longer just her playmates began to draw her fancy. Now the queen used this growing interest as a weapon with which to bludgeon our young goddess (who had all but completely forgotten who she was by now).

"Boys don't like girls who climb trees. How are you going to get a husband acting like that? Sit down, be still, be quiet, you're too loud."

It went on and on, criticism like water, dripping upon a stone. The girl was beginning to get worn down. Sometimes when she could no longer stand it she would run away. Hot tears streaming down her face she would run away into the woods and hide, but at other times she would go visit her old friend in "the tower".

She had discovered her one day when after one of her mother's fits of rage she was looking for someplace to hide. She had run from the queen's wrath not knowing where she was going, barely able to see through her tears. She ran through the kitchen and through the servant's quarters when she suddenly found herself at the foot of a narrow staircase that she had never seen before. She thought she had found a good place to take refuge so she quickly and quietly climbed the long flight of stairs. When she finally reached the landing she found herself facing a door that stood slightly ajar. She was startled to see a soft yellow light coming from within. She cautiously pushed the door open on its squeaky hinges and peered around the corner.

She nearly jumped out of her skin when her eyes met the face of an old woman with white hair drawn up in a bun on the top of her head. The old woman chuckled at her expression and beckoned her in.

"Come, come sit down." Not knowing why, she obeyed the old woman. Perhaps it was something about her kind amused eyes or her dazzling smile accented by her lovely pink lipstick.

The girl wondered at her beauty. Until then she had always thought this sort of beauty belonged only to youth but she now saw differently. She was also a bit portly, as the girl would imagine a grandmother to be. She had to imagine because she did not have a grandmother of her own. She had learned from the servants that her own grandmother, Isabel had been banished from the kingdom by her mother many years ago upon her great uncle's death and her mother's subsequent ascendancy to the throne. She never did learn what the offense was that led to the banishment nor where the woman was living or if in fact she was living at all.

The girl took a seat across from the old woman, wiping away her tears, as she looked about the cozy little warm room. The old woman regarded the girl for a moment, a look of pleasure spreading across her face before asking.

"Who troubled you?"

This was the first but not to be the last time the little girl would hear this from her friend but for some reason upon hearing this question, she just burst into tears and told the old woman everything. She told her about the fits of her mother, and her attempts to break her spirit and she told her how she feared that she would never be able to please the queen, let alone get her to love her. It all just poured forth in one long stream of words and tears and not just a little bit of rage. The old woman reached for her, pulling the girl onto her lap, took her in her arms and held her until she was finished.

She held her and stroked her murmuring comforting words then said, "She was not always like this you know. There was a time before, a long time ago when she was kind and full of wonder just like you."

"How do YOU know this?" demanded the girl as she looked into the old woman's face. "Who are you and why are you here in this room? Are you an old servant, past your time of working?"

The old woman seemed to consider carefully before she answered. "Yes. I am an old servant. At one time I cared for your mother. I tended to all her needs. We were very close then but all that has changed now. When she no longer needed me I was assigned other duties and eventually when I became too old to work I was sent here to the tower."

"But why were you allowed to stay in the palace? All the others are sent away or go to live somewhere in the village or countryside."

The old woman regarded the child carefully again then said, "I guess your mother never really forgot who I was to her when she was a child. She has allowed me to stay here. I know to you she is only what you see now, but she could be very kind before. I also know that she loves you very much."

At this the little girl pushed the woman away slightly, saying, "NO she does not love me. She loves only herself."

The old woman just shook her head and said, "In time you may come to see that the opposite is in fact true."

The little girl did not understand and right now she did not care what was meant by this. She was hungry and tired after her outburst. The old woman gave her sweet tarts to eat and hot tea with milk. After a long nap the child awoke and the old woman sent her on her way. The child hugged her and made her way down the stairs.

She could hear the old woman whisper behind her as she descended the stairs, "Walk good."

The child laughed at her strange expression before turning to give her one last little wave at the bottom of the stairs. After that she secretly visited the old woman almost every day.

Years passed and the young girl began to blossom into a young woman. Life at the palace continued pretty much as before. The prince worked. He had an entire empire to run and a fleet of merchant ships. He often allowed Isabelle to be in attendance when he met with his advisors and she learned much about his business and the affairs of state. Her mother discouraged this as she discouraged the other sort of lessons that the prince allowed. Perhaps because he had no son, he allowed Isabelle to be trained in the arts of warfare and combat. She was adept with a sword and other weaponry, even competing in and winning many contests.

The queen, on the other hand, commanded all those in the palace. Sometimes there were parties, sometimes trips abroad, sometimes visitors from other kingdoms. Occasionally a visiting family would bring a son, a potential suitor. During these visits the princess would sit quite still as she had been taught and focus on looking pretty. She could not hide the look of utter boredom on her face and some suitors, turned off by this, would go away shaking their heads. Others, in an attempt to engage her would suggest a walk around the palace grounds. Once out from under the watchful gaze of her parents, the girl would take these young men to see her horses. Unable to resist, she would invariably change clothing and suggest a ride. Once in her element she would challenge the young men to all sorts of games, archery, riding feats etc.

Some of these men she actually quite liked and for fleeting moments she could imagine falling in love and marrying, having someone to share her adventures with, a true partner, an end to her solitude. However, she had a most ungracious and un-princess like habit of playing very hard and often won out in these competitions. After a long while she and her new "friend" would return to the drawing room, her clothes and hair a mess, her cheeks red, eyes shining. The princes, gentlemen all, would look somewhat miffed and put out and would soon thereafter take their leave saying a polite good bye to the confused princess and her royal parents.

Her mother chastised her vigorously after these lapses from lady like behavior. "You will never find a prince like this!"

The girl too wondered if she ever would find someone to love. Where was he and would he ever come?

The princess also took her lessons. Her parents hired the best teachers and had her receive instruction in all fields of study. She was continually discouraged from engaging in the old activities that she used to enjoy. Less and less did she hunt or fish or roam the woods. More and more did she dress and act as expected. The queen was pleased to see this change in her daughter. Perhaps all her efforts would pay off and the girl would yet find a husband to complete the process of domestication.

During pleasant weather, the queen would call round to the stable and have a carriage sent so she and her daughter could go for a ride through town near parliament house. During these outings the princess would sit stiffly beside her mother smiling faintly at those they passed. Her mother would chat with other ladies but was especially friendly to those rare acquaintances that had sons who would be suitable for marriage to her daughter. The princess would look on wearing an imperious expression, not unlike her mother's. She tried not to focus on her shoes that felt too tight and on the clothes that seemed ridiculous after a few hours. She also tried to ignore the immense boredom and utter loneliness that she felt.

More than a few ladies would comment to each other later, "She is quite pretty."

"Yes, like her mother, but a bit cold."

"Yes, just like her mother and I hear she is quite impossible too."

"Yes."

Less and less did she ride out in the fields. More and more time did she spend indoors. She seemed to be trading her old adventure for a different kind; adventures of the mind. She spent many hours in the library reading and studying. Her father worried about this change but her mother convinced him that this was a good thing, reminding him of how he had appreciated her mind when they met.

"She will please her husband by being able to keep up with him in conversation."

The prince seemed uncertain but he let it die. He was at least glad that Isabelle still spent time with him, accompanying him to his business meetings and on other affairs of state.

There was one other change as well. The princess rarely visited her gift anymore. The last couple of times when she had, she had a strange reaction. Rather than enjoying the mysterious power she felt ill afterward and had to lie still for a long time to recover from it. After one such episode she grew very weak and the palace doctor had to be summoned. She took ill with fever and slept for three days, only waking to drink water. After this she was in bed for a month. Even when she recovered she was very weak and wore a listless look upon her face. It was during this time that she made a curious discovery...

One day during her convalescence she was sitting in the solarium taking some sun. She was alone and un-customarily bored. Some of her old spirit of curiosity and mischief was about her so she decided to go exploring as she used to in the cellars of the castle. She stood up on her weak legs, wrapped her wool shawl more closely around her and walked to the far end of the hall where the stairs led down to the cold and dank cellar. Once down there she found the usual odd collection of cast off things, furniture, bird cages, unwanted gifts that could not be thrown out.

Then she saw something she had never noticed before. Against the wall, partially hidden by an old painted Chinese screen, she saw a medieval suit of armor. It had long since lost its shine and was dark and tarnished. It's now dull surface was dark grey, almost black in fact, but something about it was very inviting. There was a cuirass, a sort of corset under the metallic torso that was made of very sturdy black leather. It was embossed with strange markings and laced up the back.

She decided to try it on so she took it off the dummy and put it on the ground. Then she unwrapped her shawl and took off her nightgown. She knew that this piece would normally be worn over some thin material but the material had long since disappeared so she put the cold leather directly on her bare skin. A strong shiver went through her whole body when she did this. Because it laced from behind she could not manage this part so she fixed it to herself as best she could. She wanted to see how she looked so she looked around for a mirror.

She found a full length mirror leaning against the wall, moved the junk from in front of it then, using a rag, wiped away cobwebs and dust before standing before the mirror. She liked what she saw standing half naked before the glass with this unusual corset covering only her torso.

Suddenly and without warning the cuirass seemed to come alive, lacing itself up her back. At the same time, she felt instantly stronger and better than she had felt in months. She felt somehow electrified and stood up straighter, if a bit rigidly. She liked how it felt although she could not help noticing that it was a bit tight. Her breathing was not coming as easily as she would have liked. She tried to push this thought from her mind, enjoying the feeling of newfound strength instead. She turned this way and that imagining herself in the midst of a fight, standing on the prow of a ship, or riding her horse into battle.

Just as she decided that she would keep it and wear it again she heard voices coming from the floor above. Her nurse was calling for her as she descended the stairs. Not wanting to take off the corset yet not wanting to be discovered like this, she quickly pulled her night dress on over it, grabbed her shawl and headed for the stairs. Later safely in her bedroom after everyone had gone to bed she undressed again and stood before the mirror to daydream some more. Not for a very long time had she had such fun letting her imagination run wild. She did this until she let out a big yawn and realized how sleepy she was.

She began to undo the corset so she could climb in bed but something was wrong. Every time she tried to pull the free end of the string to release herself the thing tightened around her forcing her breath out of her lungs. The harder she tried the tighter it got. She tried to force it down from the top. She tore at the bottom with her now weak hands. She struggled until the thing got so tight that it threatened to cut off her air entirely! She wondered if she should call for help but knew she had better not. She panted loudly, panicked. What was happening? This could not be real. She decided to take a brief rest and try again to remove the now hateful garment. With all her strength she twisted and turned in an attempt to free herself. Finally exhausted she began to cry. Looking down in despair she could see that the thing had now become a part of her! Exhausted, she finally gave up for the night and fell asleep. Maybe she would have better luck in the morning when her strength had returned.

The next morning she awoke groggily with the sunlight streaming in the window on her face. She was recalling her horrible dream of the demon cuirass. What a nightmare! In her half sleeping state she began to stretch but stopped. Something was wrong. She put her hands on her body…no! Her hands felt the cold leather just as she looked down and saw it. It was not a dream! The black cuirass with its strange markings was still on her. She struggled for over an hour but try as she might, she could not remove it.

With a mixture of bitterness and excitement in her heart, she resigned herself to it. In some ways she liked the way it looked and especially how it felt. She felt protected by it and in a way it gave her strength; helped her to keep an erect posture; would no doubt support her when her energy flagged as it had begun to do in recent years. She also decided that she would tell no one because for some reason it shamed her and made her feel different. She had long ago grown tired of feeling different. No, she would tell no one. It would be her secret. So on that morning she rose and dressed herself, pulling her undergarments over this new feature of hers, and putting her gown on top of these, and then she slowly buttoned herself into an elegant green taffeta gown with malachite buttons. She would go for a ride in the carriage with her mother as usual.

After this, life at the palace continued pretty much as before. She continued her studies; history, political science, languages, dancing and painting. She still took her martial arts and fighting lessons but most of her time was spent in the library. Rarely did she even ride her horses and when she did it was a tame ride over the fields. No longer did she go galloping through the woods and streams, her head uncovered, muddying her clothes. She occasionally accompanied her father when he tended to the matters of the state and his business. He had acquired a new fleet of merchant ships that seemed to require much of his attention.

The queen entertained and ran the household. Occasionally suitors came but the outcome was always the same. The princess almost never visited with her gift and on the rare occasions when she did, all she would do is look at the beautiful box with the iridescent Morpho inlaid on the lid. She could no longer stand to feel the power it contained. Besides she had her magical cuirass to give her strength. What was in the box only made her feel ill.

One day, not long after her sixteenth birthday, the princess accompanied her mother to the house of one of her close acquaintains, Lady Ann Seaworthy. It was the usual gathering of ladies of the court. They were having tea in the woman's lush drawing room. The ladies were prattling on about nothing, gossip really. The princess had long ago learned to listen with only one ear just in case someone addressed her. Occasionally a question was put to her. Usually it was about her studies. She did at least enjoy relating what she was learning to whoever asked. The current subject was ornithology. The women listened with polite amusement at her excitement.

"Did you know that the colors of the peacock plumage are actually due to optical interference? Some of their color also comes from pigmentation but the really brilliant color comes from a type of iridescence. They have nearly periodically arranged miniscule bowl-shaped structures found in their feathers. The various colors correspond to different scale length of these periodic structures. For example, for brown feathers, a mixture of blue and..." One of the ladies interrupted. "I have heard that their brilliant color comes from a diet of thorns. Is this true?"

Before she could answer, the door of the drawing room burst open and their hostess turned toward it exclaiming with joy. The ladies, including our princess, turned to see what she thought was the most beautiful man that she had ever seen. He was tall. He reminded her of the outdoors. His hair was the color of dry sand and his normally light skin was suntanned. His eyes too were like summer but also held the brilliant blue of the sky. Even the oldest women in the room seemed to preen as he entered

He greeted them all warmly. "Hello ladies." Then addressing the lady of the house, "Good afternoon aunt." She stood up and he gave her a big hug.

The girl felt something she had never experienced before. She felt warm as she placed her hand on her cheek and she felt suddenly shy, something she rarely felt, and even a bit dizzy. He glanced her way and gave her a quick smile. Had the others seen that? Had she imagined it?

Almost as quickly as he came, he left. He had just arrived in town and would be staying with his aunt but did not want to interrupt their tea so he grabbed a piece of cake off the table, kissed his aunt quickly and left the room. After this the princess was very distracted. She wanted to ask her hostess about him but did not dare. She knew that this behavior was exactly the sort her mother would call aggressive so she held her tongue and waited for the others to ask. Eventually they did.

His name was Charmant and he was a prince. Apparently he was studying at a foreign university, something that had to do with finance. She could not be sure. He was here for the summer holiday visiting his aunt and her two daughters. She was delighted to hear this last bit of information. She was sure to see him again, but when? She looked up and met her mother's eyes upon her, a knowing look on her face. The girl frowned and looked away.

For the next couple of weeks she found herself in frequent daydreams about this young handsome man. She imagined riding with him, swimming in the streams and lakes in the countryside, later sitting by the fireplace with him. She could not help thinking of him all the time it seemed. One day her mother came to her and told her that they had been invited to a garden party to be held on Sunday. She was glad to have something else to think about, something to distract her from her new found obsession.

On Sunday she and her parents rode away in the summer carriage to the party. It was a perfect day; sunny but not too hot. Big white clouds billowed across the sky. A light breeze ruffled her skirts as she climbed out of the carriage in the drive of the house where the party was being held.

She had been sitting placidly looking around the garden when she noticed a small commotion. It seemed that several people were moving toward the house, specifically toward the French doors that stood open to the music room. She stood without thinking and followed the crowd. As she drew closer she could hear piano music and singing coming from within. She was not able to tell if the voice was male or female yet but something drew her to it. It was beautiful; a low almost sad tune somehow familiar and yet foreign. It awoke something inside of her, something that had gone to sleep a long time ago, long before the secret of the black cuirass, just before she had all but stopped visiting her gift.

She stood rooted to the spot enthralled by the music, she had closed her eyes to hear better. The song carried her away, back to a time of peace and innocence, back to a time when she was full of wonder. She could almost feel sunshine on her skin and hear the sounds of the forests in which she used to roam, hear the creek rushing as she rode through it on Philippides' back.

She stood like this for some time and was not even aware when the song ended. It was the sound of clapping that broke her reverie. When the crowd shifted and thinned she saw who had been at the piano. It was Charmant! He left the crowd and came to her asking if it was she that he had seen the other day at his aunt's home. After this they spent the rest of the afternoon together talking as if they were the only two in the whole world. He told her all about his studies and the foreign city in which he lived. She told him about her latest passions and about her favorite animals, going on for some time about Xerxes and Philippides. He laughed at the stories she told him of her many adventures. When the time came to part he asked if he might see her again. They were to go out the next day. He would call on her around noon.

That night she barely slept. She wondered if this is what it felt like to be in love. It felt as if a thousand tiny butterflies had invaded her stomach. When her breakfast was brought to her in the morning she could not eat it. As the hour drew near she heard a knock on her door. She gave a start as she thought perhaps he had arrived early and she was not fully dressed yet. She was surprised to see her mother enter the room. She had come to admonish her. She warned her to stay away from her usual un-lady like behavior, reminding her that she was a princess and that she should conduct herself as such at all times.

"It is unbecoming to be so eager and please do not get out there and run wild. Men do not like women who act wild or are loud and boisterous. You should be quiet and demure and undemanding."

The princess suggested that perhaps it was better for her to be herself but her mother interrupted her.

"You have plenty of time to be you later. I'm just saying don't scare him off. I'm not suggesting that you not be you but perhaps you could just be a little less you. I've told you many times, men do not want a woman who draws attention to herself. They want a woman who helps them shine, who makes them look good. Just trust me."

The daughter did not really trust her mother but then her mother did have her father and he was a charming handsome prince so perhaps she should listen. Isabelle made a promise to herself to be demure.

Prince Charmant arrived exactly on time riding in a lovely carriage of the deepest mahogany with accents of burnished leather and copper. There were two black horses pulling it and there were two white horses, already saddled, attached by leads to its rear. As they pulled off she asked him where they were going. He told her that it was a surprise.

They rode along in relative silence both smiling, looking out the windows, taking in the almost perfect day. There were many things she wanted to ask him about himself, but she concentrated on the passing scenery, feeling it was better to let him ask the questions, lest she appear any more eager than she already had. Occasionally she turned toward him to find him looking at her. When their eyes met she quickly looked away. As the carriage rode on she noticed that they were entering territory that was unfamiliar to her. This surprised her as she thought she knew every inch of the kingdom. They were now passing through a large open field. She was delighted to see that it was filled with wildflowers of the most brilliant pinks, purples, blues and yellows. She wanted so much to get out here and collect all the flowers she could. Just when she could contain herself no longer and was about to ask to stop, the driver came to a halt in the middle of this beautiful field. Had he read her thoughts? They left the carriage here and mounted the horses. He offered her a leg up, and forgetting her promise to herself to be demure, ignored him and mounted the horse without his help. The princess was excited feeling some of her old sense of adventure returning.

They walked the horses at a comfortable pace through the field of wildflowers enjoying the sunshine and sweet smells in the warm, dry air. Presently they came to the edge of a wood and entered its cool dark interior. She stole a look at the prince. She was so happy, being on an adventure with this handsome prince. A few months ago she never would have imagined this; being with a young handsome prince, a man who was clearly interested in her.

The woods seemed to be alive. Birds and other small animals darted everywhere. She saw several Zebra Swallowtail butterflies, her favorites. She delighted in their irregular flight pattern. After some time she began to wonder again about their destination. She asked Charmant if they had a particular destination in mind. He asked her if she was growing impatient and told her if she was then they could hurry. Before she could even open her mouth to respond he kicked his horse hard and took off with a whoop. She stood startled for one moment, then followed suit. She caught up to him quickly but he did not slow down. It had become a race although she did not know where the finish line was.

They galloped through the forest, jumping over fallen trees and small creeks. She felt happy; alive and exhilarated. They tore on through the dark green interior of the forest, both focused only on the terrain in front of them and on reaching the unforeseen finish line. The two horses could be heard breathing hard. All four of them, the horses and their riders had worked up a sweat. Just when she began to think that she could not go on any further, the prince started to lag and she happily pulled ahead of him.

She was becoming aware of a sort of dull roar in the air around them and vaguely wondered what it was. Eventually the roar became clearer and she realized that it was the sound of rushing water. Just then they broke into a large emerald clearing. The princess pulled back sharply on the reins as she saw where they had come to. They could go no further. Both horses came to a rather abrupt stop panting hard, sweating. The princess walked her horse slowly to the edge of the clearing and found herself looking down into a deep ravine. They had come to the top of Crystal Falls and the sight was breathtaking. She sat atop her horse for a long while just surveying the scenery and breathing in the cool, moist air. It smelled green and wet and lush.

The prince moved up slowly beside her. She looked over to see him smiling at her. He looked very pleased as he said, "So what do you think? Was it worth the wait?"

She only smiled broadly in reply.

They dismounted then and he tied the horses to a nearby tree where they could drink from the stream and graze on fresh grass. He then unloaded their saddle bags and spread out a lavish feast on a quilt. In the center he placed a small copper vase and filled it with a bouquet of the bright wildflowers from the field.

She looked quizzically at the flowers. "When did you pick those? I never saw you do that."

He beamed at her. "I picked them when we first stopped. You were in the carriage."

He took her hand and bid her to sit down on the quilt. She did so, first taking off her boots. Then they ate, at first in silence, just looking around the wood and taking in the beauty then he spoke.

"You're different than I remember. I guess the tomboy has finally become the proper princess."

She was surprised and looked at him, her brow furrowed, trying to recall when they had met before. She stiffened almost imperceptibly before saying in a cool tone, "I'm sorry but have I met you before?"

He chuckled as he answered "Not only did you know me, you used to torture me on an almost daily basis!"

"I'm sorry," she said, "but you are going to have to tell me what you are talking about."

Now he laughed aloud. "Yes I guess I will. I suppose I was just one of your many victims. I was a shy boy, small for my age, and no doubt made very little impression on you. We used to play together as children. You were always picking on me for some reason or another. You actually beat me up on a few occasions. I somehow convinced myself that you picked on me because you secretly fancied me!"

It was now her turn to laugh. She vaguely remembered the prince now. He had been a scrawny child and somewhat timid.

"Maybe I did secretly like you or maybe you just got on my nerves. I'm so sorry if I tortured you though. I was a bit of a bully at times. I hope you can forgive me."

"Oh I forgave you a long time ago. You actually helped me quite a bit."

"I did? How so?"

"Well for one thing every time you beat me in some game or another my friends teased me mercilessly. I vowed to get better and to one day garner the respect of my peers. I guess I used you and those times as a sort of reminder of who I never wanted to be again."

Although he spoke lightly, she could see the hurt of the former little boy and was truly sorry then.

Her tone was more serious as she explained. "Although I did not show it, I was often unhappy as a child. Let's just say being Cythona's daughter was not always fun. I am not trying to make excuses but looking back I really think I often took it out on the other children. I am truly sorry."

The prince brushed it off. "Really I'm okay. Look at me. I'm all grown up now." This last bit he said with a mischievous laugh straightening up and striking a regal pose.

She smiled at him searching his face for any traces of the pain she had caused him. Finding none she shook her head pushed her empty wine glass toward him and said, "Well then let's move on. A toast to a fresh start?"

He nodded in agreement and they raised their glasses.

Then in a more sober tone he looked in her eyes. "Actually you really did have an effect on me in another way as well"

He confessed to her then that he had always had a crush on her but as a child and as a young man he was afraid to let her know. Her wildness and her brash manner had scared him before now and he felt that she would never return his affections and that he would only be embarrassed were he to express his true feelings. He had vowed to make himself into the sort of man that she would respect and admire. He had grown into a very handsome man and had finally become very popular both with his peers and young women. He also confessed that he often asked his aunt for news of her and news of almost everything that she had gone through over the past several years that they had not seen one another. He heard the gossip about her wild ways and her mother's every attempt to marry her off to some suitor or another.

He knew too of her mother's growing concern of ever finding someone suitable for her daughter. He knew about her studies, her hobbies and he knew too that she spent most of her time alone, not really fitting in with the other ladies on the court. Finally he confessed that he had decided to spend his summer holiday with his aunt to be close to her.

This was all too much for her somehow and she suddenly felt embarrassed, exposed and very vulnerable. She accused him of exaggerating and tried to make some joke or another, "Come on. Let's stop this serious talk. We came out here to have fun."

He looked at her, surprised by her reaction but did not waver. "I am not exaggerating," he said emphatically "I think I'm in love with you!" then more quietly "I think I have always been in love with you."

She only stared at him, unsure of what to say next. She was saved by Mother Nature. Just then a Zebra Swallowtail flitted in between them and came to rest on the flowers in the vase that rested on the blanket.

"Oh look," she exclaimed. "Have you ever seen a Zebra Swallowtail before?"

He looked at her, somewhat annoyed answering coolly. "No I can't say I have."

Undaunted by his obvious change in mood, she went on. "Well this has always been one of my favorites. I used to collect butterflies when I was little. I wonder if I can still catch one."

At this she stretched out her hand slowly. The butterfly, feasting on the nectar of the wildflowers was in a sort of trance, her wings opening and closing slowly, rhythmically. The prince noted the rapt attention on her face as she stretched just a little closer then using her index finger and thumb, pinched the butterfly's wings together gently, stopping their opening and closing. She smiled broadly then and looking at the prince held the butterfly out as if she was holding a trophy. In spite of himself, he had to laugh. She placed the creature on his arm and they both watched it for a moment before it flitted off again. After it was out of sight the prince suggested that they go exploring.

They spent the rest of the afternoon walking through the woods, climbing over fallen trees and moss covered boulders.

They followed the stream for a time and came upon a pool, deep and clear, perfect for swimming but when Prince Charmant suggested they swim, the princess, terrified of revealing the corset, said "But I don't have my bathing costume, I can't swim in my dress."

The prince suggested an obvious alternative to the bathing suit.

She just rolled her eyes and suggested that perhaps they ought to be getting back as it was late. They walked in relative silence back to the picnic spot and packed up as the sun made her way toward the western sky. They rode out of the forest, which was almost dark now and back across the field in the gathering summer dusk. They made pleasant conversation in the carriage ride, recalling the highlights of the day. When he dropped her off at the palace he held her hand as he walked her to the door. She was self conscious, aware of how hot her hand must have felt to his.

He bent and kissed her lightly on the cheek before holding her away from him to look into her eyes. "I meant what I said in the forest today. I very much want to see you again. May I?"

All but forgetting her promise to herself earlier, she said eagerly "I would like that very much."

The princess practically floated to her chamber that night, dressed for bed in a dream like state and slept peacefully.

She was awakened abruptly by her mother who was full of questions. What time did you get home, what did you do and worst of all, how did you behave? None of her answers did the queen find acceptable. When she learned of their wild ride she admonished the princess that she had no doubt scared Charmant off.

The princess retorted peevishly, "Then why did he ask to see me again?"

"Because that is what men do. What did you expect him to say? They will say what they think you want to hear. Stop being so naive! What did you say when he asked you if you wanted to see him again?"

For a moment she considered lying to her mother then said quietly, "I said yes."

Her mother let out a snort then, "Of course you did."

"Why wouldn't I say 'yes'? I do want to see him again."

"Because men like to chase, that's why. How many times do I have to tell you that? When you appear too eager it turns them off. I made your father wait a very long time before I agreed to let him court me."

She thought but did not say "Poor daddy." Instead she said "But I don't want to play games. Besides the prince is not like that. He likes me as I am!"

"Really?" That dangerous tone had crept into her mother's voice. "Really? He likes you as you are huh? Men will say and do anything to get you to believe that. Don't! Trust me. Make him chase you. If he really likes you he will stick around. Right now all you have done is scare him off."

After this her mother ordered her to get up. They were to go shopping in the town. She wanted to say "no", that she had no interest in going anywhere with her mother. Her stomach was in knots, her mind a whirl thinking about every word she had said to Charmant, thinking of the prince repulsed by her, pretending to like her. She felt shamed and just wanted to stay in her room by herself, but before she could say anything her mother barked. "Hurry up! Get up; we are leaving in half an hour!" She walked out then slamming the door behind her.

In the carriage Isabelle sat stiffly next to her mother. They did their usual rounds through the town, greeting other ladies and their daughters, stopping in several shops. She usually just took a seat in the corner while her mother tried on clothes and picked over jewelry, sometimes buying something, sometimes not. Occasionally her mother persuaded her to try on something. The princess was in no mood but she submitted to this, all the while feeling bored and looking listless.

In one shop Isabelle was trying on a hat. As she regarded her expression in the mirror she thought she caught a glimpse of a familiar face in the glass of the shop window. Her heart jumped and she turned in time to see Charmant walking past the shop next to a young woman that she recognized as one of the girls from the garden party. A girl she did not know but whom she had seen a few times before. The girl clung to his arm in a most irritating way. Without thinking she ran to the shop window and watched them walking away. The pair entered a small restaurant on the corner. She turned back slowly toward the interior of the shop and met her mother's scornful gaze.

"Oh well."

The girl was enraged but only said, "What does that mean?"

"It means 'oh well'. There are plenty of fish in the sea. What did you expect? Don't worry about him. Next time maybe you will do as I tell you."

After this the queen turned away from her and took up a conversation with her lady in waiting. She told her what to have sent to the palace. Then they went to lunch at the same place where she had seen the prince go but he was nowhere to be seen. The princess barely ate and could not wait to get home to the privacy of her chamber.

When they finally got home after what seemed like hours, the princess practically ran to her room. Once safely inside the door, she threw herself on the bed and began to cry. She cried for sometime before sitting up and wiping her eyes. She looked calmly around her chamber now, watching the late afternoon sun stream through the windows, watching the dust swirl in the sunbeams. She wiped at her nose with the back of her sleeve with a sniff. Maybe her mother was right after all. What did being herself get her? The prince was clearly not interested. But then why would he have said those things to her in the woods? She could almost hear her mother's voice, "because that's what men do."

She got up, resolving to move on with her day. She needed to move. She changed into her riding pants, boots and a man's shirt and called for Xerxes.

She hugged him to herself, "Hey good boy, you're a good boy, you're MY good boy."

They wrestled about for a minute before she rose and dusted herself off. They headed out into the warm early summer dusk, stopping to admire the lush greenery of the countryside from the terrace before heading to the barn. She greeted Philippides, who was happy to see her, having not seen her in some time. She scratched and tugged at his mane for a few moments before quickly saddling him, mounting and setting off. They rode out into the fields, going nowhere in particular. It was an easy ride. They alternately walked, trotted then galloped through the countryside.

She could feel that Philippides was restless and wanted, like her, to blow off some steam, so as they entered a wide open field she kicked his sides and set him to an all out gallop. She reveled in the feeling of the warm, sweet air rushing past her head, filling her nose and lungs with it. The night was gathering now and the moon was rising above the hills before them. They rode on like this for some time. She noted that poor Xerxes was beginning to flag and knew he could not keep up for much longer.

"Just a minute more boy." she called to him as they took the small hill before them. As they neared the top she slowed and then brought Philippides to a halt. The three of them stood there silhouetted by the moon. She looked down on the valley before her, the cottages and landscape bathed in silver moonlight. She admired the beauty of it all and had all but forgotten about the prince by the time she turned and headed back to the castle.

She kept to herself for the next few days, spending her days in the library or painting in her studio. She loved to paint in the bright sunlight just after noon. As the dusk was gathering she would repeat the ritual of that night on the hill. Sometimes Xerxes would accompany her and Philippides, and other times he would choose to stay close to home, avoiding the arduous journey.

It was on the fifth night after the incident at the shop that something unexpected happened. It was a particularly hot night. She had been restless that day, finding it hard to concentrate on her studies owing to the oppressive heat. So after exercising Philippides, she stripped him of his saddle, stripped herself of her riding togs, and they all went for a swim.

Xerxes had deigned to come with her so he too got to go for a swim. She stayed on Philippides' back, holding onto his mane, feeling the cool water drift over them. It was pure heaven feeling the soft water caress her skin. Xerxes chased ducks along the bank, splashing happily.

After the swim she lay on a rock to dry. It was still warm from the day's heat and she enjoyed the warmth on her bare skin. Closing her eyes, she lay there for some time. Something gentle made her open her eyes. It was a clear moonless night so she gazed into a black sky and could see almost every constellation. A shooting star blazed across the canopy of the sky just then and she found herself making a silent wish on it. She wished for her prince, someone to share all this beauty with. After this she lay on her side for awhile listening to the crickets and luxuriating in the summer night. Then she dressed, saddled Philippides, woke Xerxes and headed home.

As she rode into the drive she saw a strange carriage parked there. It was rather late for visitors. Maybe her father had important business. She hoped nothing was wrong. She had a vague feeling of worry as she rode on past the drive to the barn. She left Philippides with the stable boy and entered the house from the back terrace. She heard laughter coming from the drawing room and as she drew closer she could make out the voice of her mother and then her friend, Lady Seaworthy. "Yes we just got back from the house on the coast. I told Charmant it was too late to call but he insisted."

The queen replied in her most gracious voice, "Oh not at all my dear. We are happy to see you and your dear niece and nephew."

The princes came around the corner and her heart nearly stopped. There sat the prince next to the girl she had seen him with the other day. She stared for a moment before her mother's voice broke her trance. "Oh dear you remember Charmant? And this is his cousin Lilly. She is visiting with her aunt for the summer too."

The princess extended her hand slowly, feeling somewhat self conscious in her dirty riding pants and shirt, her hair a mess. She barely glanced at the prince before taking a seat across from them on the couch next to her mother. Xerxes tried to jump up on the couch to take his seat next to her, but the princess gently pushed him off the couch then sat stroking his head.

Then Charmant spoke to her. "So how have you been?" Nothing in his tone gave away whether he knew what she had gone through for the past five days. She said that she had been well and inquired about him.

She learned then, that his cousin had arrived the day after their picnic and they had set off on an impromptu holiday to their villa on the coast. "We had a great time. You should come next time we go. Lilly doesn't know too many people here so it would have been good for her. We are away at school together. We decided to go at the last minute or I would have asked you."

Lilly agreed. She was a charming girl.

Now that she had a closer look the princess could easily see the family resemblance.

Lady Seaworthy spoke. "Well we really have to get going now. It's very late." Then she shot Isabelle a knowing look before saying. "Charmant really insisted that we stop but we must be going now. Isabelle when will you come to see us? I know Charmant and Lilly would like this very much."

The next day Charmant came to call and almost every day after that they were together. Sometimes Lilly accompanied them, but most times they were alone. It was an idyllic summer; riding their horses over almost every inch of the kingdom, swimming at Crystal Falls, and the occasional weekend at the coast. There were several parties, dances in the moonlight. Every moment apart was a torture and she looked forward to the moments when they would be together. She no longer felt alone. One day in late summer they rode their horses to Mr. Butler's farm. The berries were ripe and they went to pick them. They lay in the grass, eating the hot sweet berries and kissing. He had suddenly grabbed her to him almost violently and asked "Why won't you say it?"

She did not know what he meant "Say what? What are you talking about?"

"You know what I mean. You never say 'I love you.' I love you and I've told you but you never say it to me. Do you not love me?"

The princess demurred, saying "I don't know what that means. I feel for you a lot but why do I have to say it?"

Then after a long pause she said quietly, "Yes, I suppose I do love you."

She had said it and she meant it. She realized in that moment that she had been afraid but that yes she had come to truly love the prince.

After this day they spoke of their future often. He was to return to school and finish in two years. They planned to marry then. They would tell no one of their engagement. He thought it better to wait, to avoid the prying eyes and minds of the lords and ladies of the court for as long as they could. The princess was ecstatic and more than happy to keep this delicious secret to herself.

One very hot, late summer afternoon Isabelle and Charmant were off riding. They had raced to the base of the falls, one of their favorite things to do. Sweating, they had just dismounted their horses when it began to rain. It was one of those hot summer rains that you don't run from. He had suddenly taken her in his arms and began to kiss her wildly. Then he undressed and ran into the clear pool beckoning for her to follow him. For a moment she was frozen. She had never been naked in front of him, or any man for that matter. It was not her nudity that worried her but the terrible secret of her quirass that she had managed to hide from everyone.

She stripped off her pants and riding jacket, leaving on her shirt and ran into the pool after him. Once there, they continued kissing, splashing, and writhing around in the water. Things were really starting to heat up when a loud clap of thunder rang out in the forest. The horses were getting spooked and pulling at their leads when a streak of lightning hit a tree not ten yards from them. Without a word they scrambled out of the pool, pulled on their soaking clothes, mounted their horses and sped away. They rode up to the Seaworthy's house panting and out of breath. They entered the foyer laughing and exclaiming at their good fortune to have gotten out of the woods before being struck by lightning. Their voices echoed off the walls. A male servant entered the hall and in one breath Charmant asked him to make up a fire in the small parlor and inquired about his aunt and cousins. He was informed that they had all gone out.

Charmant took Isabelle's hand then and led her into the parlor. He poured some brandy for her and handing her a towel turned to pour one for himself. She wrapped the towel around her shoulders and went and stood before the fire sipping her drink slowly. He came up behind her and lifting the towel off her shoulders began to dry her hair. He took fresh towels and dried her from head to toe before beginning to take off her jacket. Between the brandy and the growing heat she found it hard to resist.

He pulled her to the floor and helped her out of her pants. She shivered a bit then. He noticed her empty glass and got up and poured her another then placed the bottle on the floor next to them before the fire place. She sat sipping from her glass as he undressed. She was hugging her knees to her chest, watching him lay their clothes on the iron screen on the hearth. The firelight dancing off of his honey colored skin. She was burning up when he took the glass from her hand and began to unbutton her shirt. She pushed his hand away and shook her head. He kissed her on the mouth and she returned the kisses. He tried again to unbutton her shirt and again she resisted.

He held her away from him to look into her eyes. He asked her, "Don't you trust me? I thought you loved me."

How could she explain that it was not what he thought? She tried to convince him that she did trust him and that she did love him but she was afraid that he would not love her if he understood.

"Understood what Isabelle? I love you and nothing can change that. Please you have to trust me?"

She finally relented and let him undress her completely. He lay there quietly for a time looking at the odd contraption. She was terrified then, terrified that what she thought was true. He would not, could not, love her now that he knew her terrible secret; the ugly "garment" that she wore, worse that she needed to wear. She began to cry. This seemed to break him out of his reverie.

Looking confused he gathered her into his arms. He asked her why she was crying. She poured out the entire story of the dreaded quirass to him concluding with her fear that discovery by him would lead him to reject her. He laughed gently at her then. He explained that this changed nothing, that he loved her and always would. He kissed away her tears. He held himself over her and she smiled into his eyes, now the color of sea glass. She ran her hands through his sandy curls and hugged him to her. He whispered into her ear "I love you."

She had never made love with a man before. She was scared and excited, anticipating what was about to happen. Just then they heard a loud knock at the door. He jumped up pulling on his clothes hastily. She tried to do the same as he moved toward the closed parlor door. She imagined the door opening at any moment and his aunt and cousins entering the room to find her, but when he did finally open the door, after waiting for her to dress, there was no one there! He called out to see if anyone was near and looked around but found no one.

After this fright, the mood was broken. They sat warming themselves by the fire until the rain stopped, which it did a short while after, then he called the carriage and took her home. They did not speak of what had happened.

The summer passed pleasantly. Isabelle and the prince spending all of their time together; attending parties, boating, riding, moonlit swims and going for long walks. Isabelle also spent occasional afternoons with the old woman in the tower. She had told her all about him and enjoyed the older woman's delight at her stories. She was the only one that the girl confided in that she and the prince were engaged and to be married once he finished his studies. The old woman had cried then. Isabelle promised her that when she and the prince married they would take her to live with them.

As the summer was drawing to a close, the princess began to worry. She did not look forward to the pain of parting from Charmant. He assured her that he would visit often and would see her during every holiday from school. All too soon their last night together arrived. The queen and the prince were away on official business. Isabelle and Charmant were to dine alone in the castle. They took their meal in the east parlor seated before the fire place. It was a warm moonlit night and the doors were thrown open to the terrace. The room was lit only by candlelight and the light from the fire but the silver light of the full moon made it seem like daylight outside.

After dinner Charmant and Isabelle went outside and lay side by side on a chaise. They lay there for a long while gazing out over the lawn listening to the late summer song of the crickets and the sound of water falling from the enormous fountain that was before them at the bottom of the steps. There was very little breeze so they decided to cool themselves by taking a dip in the fountain. It was a childish thing to do and they had fun wading and splashing in the moonlight. They emerged cool and happy, dressed and took up their seats again on the terrace. Isabelle told him of the night she wished on the star for him. He said that he too had wished for her and that being with her was like a long held dream come true. They lay here for a very long time, neither one of them wanting the night to end. There were many tears and long embraces as the dawn broke violently in the east. She walked him out to his carriage that stood waiting in the drive. They parted with kisses and promises to be together again soon. She stood in the open doorway and watched until his carriage went down the long drive and out of sight.

She called to Xerxes who had been sleeping by the fire and went up to bed. She woke late in the afternoon to find that her parents had returned. She joined them for lunch, feeling quite content and happy. It was during lunch that a servant came to the door bearing a large bouquet of wildflowers, the same variety that they he had picked from the field that first day. Her mother made a snide remark about the unusual choice of blooms, but the princess smiled to herself. Charmant knew her and what she liked and loved her for who she was.

Prince Helios excused himself from the table saying that he was tired. Isabelle noted that he had not been looking very well lately. Moving more slowly, his usually lively step diminished somehow. He asked Isabelle to accompany him to his study. He wanted to speak to her about something. Looking at him and having taken note of his less than perfect health she was concerned about what he might wish to say to her.

Once in his study, he bade her to sit down. He inquired about how her summer had been and how her studies were coming along. She happily reported all of this to him to include some of the time that she had spent with Charmant. Of course she did not tell him about their secret engagement. The prince spoke, a note of concern in his deep voice.

"Isabelle, what are the prince's intentions with you?"

She was caught off guard, "His intentions, what do you mean? He is in love with me." And more quietly, "I assume from things that he has said that he wishes to marry me."

"Did he ask you to marry him?"

"No, not yet, why?"

"Isabelle, you are young and frankly sometimes you are too trusting. You have been sheltered from the world, but people are not always what they seem. I am only saying to be careful. Don't rush into anything. Do you understand me?"

Isabelle, a bit taken aback, promised that she would be careful then she changed the subject. "Father, are you alright? You seem tired lately. I'm worried about you."

The prince paused and regarded her for a moment before he spoke. He looked lovingly into her eyes, as always he saw his own eyes staring back. He told her that he was fine. He had been working very hard lately. They had recently established an island colony in the so called new world and her father's fleet ran a supply line to and from this colony, which he had named Orphalese. There had been some trouble with his fleet of merchant ships. Pirates had attacked and looted several of his vessels and made off with a small fortune. He told her that worry over this had taken its toll on him.

She asked if she could help in any way. "I can always travel for you if you need me to father. You know I'd like nothing more than to go on a mission for you."

The prince smiled at her. He had always admired his daughter's lust for adventure. "Thank you daughter but there isn't anything you can do right now, but if there is I will let you accompany me on my next trip."

Isabelle was delighted. "Okay father, well you had better rest up before we have to set sail. I want you to take better care of yourself. You work too hard and worry too much."

She hugged him then and told him how much she loved him. "I love you too Isabelle, very much."

She left him then to get some rest and finding Xerxes outside the door decided to take him for a walk around the garden where he happily chased the geese and ducks into the pond.

The next week passed without incident. Isabelle stuck close to home waiting to hear from Charmant. Every day she checked to see if a letter had arrived from him. Every day there was no letter. She tried to ignore her mother's knowing "I told you so" gaze that mocked her as attempted to feign dis-interest in the post.

After two weeks with no letter, Isabelle could take it no longer so one night she sat down at her desk and wrote Charmant a long letter. She inquired about his studies and his friends and told him everything she had been up to since he left. She told him about her father's troubles with the fleet, of her adventures with Xerxes and Philippides. She told him how she missed him and longed to see him, being careful not to say too much about this lest she appear overly eager. She concluded her letter with love and asked him to write back "If you have time."

Two weeks later a letter finally came from him. It came during lunch. She sat in the dining room with her parents for as long as she could after lunch before taking up the letter off the sideboard and running to her room to read it. Once in her room she locked the door, jumped on the bed, and tore open the letter.

The letter, one page written on heavy stationary in impeccable handwriting read...

> *Dear Isabelle,*
>
> *Thank you very much for your letter. I am doing well. School has taken up a great deal of my concentration this term. I am struggling with some advanced economic classes and barely have time to visit with my friends. I look forward to the end of school when I can leave this place behind and begin my real life. I am not sure if I will be able to visit my aunt in the fall. I had lunch with Lilly the other day. She told me to give you her regards.*
>
> *All the best,*
>
> *Charmant*

She sat staring at the letter. What was this? Perhaps he was concerned that her mother might be reading her letters and had not wanted to be too revealing? But surely he could have said more than this! She tried to tell herself that there was a good explanation for this sort of letter so why did she have a nagging feeling in her stomach? No, she would not jump to conclusions. She must have faith. His feelings for her could not have changed that quickly. What about their wonderful summer? They had spent nearly every day together. He had professed his love for her. He wanted to marry her! Didn't he?

Two more weeks passed with no word from him or of him. She tried her best not to worry but she did not sleep well during this time and often seemed distracted. She walked around in a daze, a worried expression on her face. Her father was concerned. Her mother knew no other letters came and noted her daughter's strange behavior, but she said nothing. In fact, she acted as if nothing whatsoever was wrong.

As the leaves began to turn, an invitation arrived for a luncheon at Lady Anne Seaworthy's house. Although Isabelle was in no mood to attend a luncheon party she agreed to go, hoping to get some news of Charmant. Surely he had asked after her to his aunt, and Lady Anne, always fond of Isabelle, would let her know this.

When the occasion for lunch came, Isabelle sat among the other ladies saying very little. She had not been eating well and a few of the ladies remarked on her weight loss. She only managed a wan smile and a remark about a diet.

They had been there for over an hour and Isabelle, unable to stand it any longer was about to inquire about Charmant when one of the ladies spoke up, "So lady Anne, I hear there is to be a wedding in your family."

Lady Anne glanced at Isabelle before answering, "Well Helene I don't believe a date has been set yet."

Lady Helene, not about to be daunted said, "Well from what I hear this has been a very long engagement. They had to have set a date by now. If I know the young lady's mother, it will be sooner rather than later. I hear she is rather annoyed that it took so long for Charmant to make the engagement public."

It was as if the air had been sucked out of the room. More than a couple of the ladies stole furtive glances at Isabelle, whose face had gone quite red. She could do nothing but stare straight ahead as the conversation swirled around her. On more than one occasion Lady Anne attempted to steer the conversation in a different direction but the talk raged on.

Apparently, Prince Charmant had been engaged to the daughter of a foreign king for the past year. He and the young woman had met when he was traveling three summers ago and began a long distance courtship. He visited her country on most of his holidays but this summer she had been traveling with her family. From all accounts this princess was stunning. She was heir to her father's throne, having no siblings, but she had no intention of truly ruling her country. Apparently she wanted a husband for this and the prince fit her profile perfectly. She much preferred the idea of being queen than actually doing the work of a ruler. She had spent her entire childhood being prepared for this role. She eschewed scholarly studies preferring to perfect the art of being a figurehead.

Isabelle sat in stony silence and was only vaguely aware that a question was being directed toward her. It was Lady Silvia. "...well Isabelle should know. Isabelle, you seem to have been quite friendly with Charmant. Do you know anything about when and where the wedding is to be?"

Her face burned as all heads turned toward her. She blinked slowly for a moment then cleared her throat. Affecting a light and disinterested tone she managed a quiet, "No you know, I don't know. He mentioned her to me, of course, but I... I don't know."

The queen broke in before it could go on any longer. "Isabelle and Charmant were friends but as a gentleman Charmant would have hardly discussed the details of his engagement with her."

"Well I just thought," said Lady Silvia "that she might know something."

Isabelle was relieved when Lady Anne finally managed to change the subject. She could barely endure the rest of the lunch but she did. On the way home in the carriage Isabelle sat staring blankly out the window; tears brimming in her eyes, which had now turned the color of the sea before a storm. Her mother had been going on for some time about the food at the lunch and what the other ladies had worn, said and done when Isabelle could take it no more.

Tears began to stream down her face and she turned to her mother "How can you just sit there going on about the stupid lunch? Do you have nothing to say about Charmant's despicable behavior?"

Cythona was taken aback "What are you talking about? What behavior? You mean being friends with you while being engaged to someone else? That is not a crime. Did he make you some promises? Did he lie to you in some way?"

"Yes! He told me he loved me! He said he wanted to be with me…said he would wait for me! I was in love with him and my heart is breaking and you sit there prattling on about the luncheon as if nothing happened!?"

"Oh don't be silly." Her mother scolded. "If he really lied to you as you said then he is hardly worth your tears. Is he? Isabelle I have told you over and over. Men will say what they feel they have to, to get what they want. He was here for the summer and wanted someone to have fun with."

"Am I being silly mother? He said he wanted to marry me."

"Well he could not have meant it. You should not have taken him seriously. No one can fall in love over one summer. He probably had feelings for you, was fond of you, but he could not have been in love, well obviously he wasn't, was he or he wouldn't be marrying someone else now would he?"

This last comment struck Isabelle's heart like a knife. "No I guess you're right. How could he have loved me?"

"Oh Isabelle. Stop being so dramatic. You are young. There will be plenty more like him. These things happen, but they are nothing to get worked up about. You are a lady and above all you are a princess. Don't let this affect you and certainly if you see him again don't ever let on that you have given your time with him a second thought. Act as if it meant nothing to you as it clearly meant nothing to him."

Isabelle truly felt as if something inside her was dying. She rode the rest of the way in silence and when she got home she ran to her room. Without bothering to undress she threw herself on the bed and cried bitterly. She cried for a long time only quieting when she heard her door opening. Xerxes having heard the noise had come up to check on her. He jumped on the bed and began to lick her tear-streaked face. She pushed him away angrily and then felt sorry. She sat up and hugged him to her continuing to cry softly. Eventually she got up, changed her clothes, washed her face and went to visit the old crone in the tower.

Once there she poured everything out to her. She cried all over again and the old woman hugged her to her breast. She listened to it only commenting every now and then but mainly she just listened and rocked the child. Isabelle told her of her mother's reaction.

"How could she say that? She knows I loved him. I feel like my heart is breaking."

The old woman held her away from her then and wiped her face. "Isabelle. Your mother is doing the best she can." Then more quietly "Maybe in some ways it's my fault."

"Your fault what do you mean? How can it be your fault?"

The old woman looked at her long and hard as if she was trying to decide something. Then it seemed that she had made a decision. "I just mean if I had taught her better…I don't know what I meant…never mind."

The girl was confused but she was also very tired now. She was emotionally spent. The old woman offered her some tea and sweets (which the girl declined) then put her to lie down. Isabelle fell into a very deep sleep and when she awoke it was nighttime and the old woman had gone to bed. She rose quietly and tiptoed through the cold castle halls toward the family's private chambers. On an impulse she entered her father's study. It was dark except for a small lamp on the desk. She approached the wall and pulled back the heavy amethyst curtain to reveal the small tabernacle there. As she had done so many times in the past she removed the jeweled box and gazed at its sparkling exterior. She traced the butterfly with her finger. Tears welled up in her eyes and splashed on the cold surface as traces of memory came to her. She cried for her childhood and for her former innocence and freedom.

She remembered with some bitterness the time before she had discovered the cuirass. How she would give anything to return to that time. She attempted to do then what she had not done in a very long time. She opened the box but when she did, was blown away by the power that emanated from it. It was as if with her neglect the power had only grown stronger while she had grown weaker. She stumbled backward and the box fell from her hands with a crash onto the stone floor. It fell on its lid, closing the box tightly. She scrambled to her feet rushing to lift the box from the floor. After inspecting it to be sure it had suffered no damage, she quickly replaced it in the alcove, closed the door and drew the curtains before quietly exiting the room. She was confused and somewhat troubled by what had happened. She went to her room, undressed and fell into a very troubled sleep.

Late autumn was now upon them and she passed the next few weeks her mood alternating between, sorrow, rage and acceptance of what had happened. She contemplated writing angry letters to Charmant demanding an explanation. She imagined going to him and confronting him in person. Those fantasies always ended in some sort of delicious revenge. Eventually these fantasies became fewer. Her tears began to dry up and as the rivers and streams began to freeze, her tears ceased to flow entirely.

Where there had been pain and grief there was now just a dull, empty spot. Life and her studies resumed and things were pretty much as they had been before Charmant. By now not one single leaf remained on the trees. Winter, which could no longer be denied, was upon them. The animals of the forest went into hibernation and a quiet coldness, like death, settled over the entire countryside.

She spent most of her days reading and writing in the library by the fireplace and the afternoons out riding or walking with Xerxes. It was on one of these afternoons after returning from a ride when she entered the house to find everyone in a panic. She was told that her father, the prince, had collapsed during a meeting with one of the commanders of the fleet. He had been taken to his chambers and the palace doctor summoned. She rushed to his rooms to find many people in attendance. Her father lay upon the bed, his eyes closed. He was unconscious and her mother stood nearby, with a tense expression on her face. She was speaking in hushed tones to the doctor. From what Isabelle could gather the doctor was saying that it had something to do with his heart, but Isabelle suspected that this illness emanated from a place that was much deeper and infinitely darker.

She went and sat on the edge of the bed and looked into her father's face. She was shocked to see how aged he looked. Although a man of about seventy, he had always looked young for his age, bright and smiling. She took his hand in hers. He opened his eyes then and smiled weakly at her. They looked into each other's eyes, neither one speaking. They did not need to.

The prince recovered slightly from this attack in three days but was to spend the next few weeks confined to his bed. She and the queen took turns sitting with him. When the queen was not by his side, she was in a frenzy, having hushed tense exchanges with her royal advisors. From what Isabelle overheard she imagined her mother was readying affairs of state in the eventuality of the prince's death. Although she was worried for her father she had no doubt that he would recover. He was a strong man with an even stronger spirit. Even when his illness dragged on and he seemed to deteriorate more each day she felt hopeful that he would recover by the spring.

There were other troubles brewing as well. The increasingly frequent attacks on their ships by pirates and her father's illness were weakening her country. Her father's most trusted captain, Admiral Gravely, who was responsible for overseeing the safe passage of their merchant fleet, was then killed while bringing precious cargo back to Xamayca from Orphalese. It was rumored that the dreaded pirate Captain Flint was responsible, but no one could be sure, because not a man had been left to tell the true account and no one had been able to bring Flint to justice. Without the prince, no one dared to make the voyage between Xamayca and the colony, and the inhabitants, cut off from much needed supplies, were dying. If things did not change soon there would be no colony to speak of and the strength of the empire might not recover.

Isabelle felt certain that she could command their fleet if given a chance but she did not dare mention such a thing. Besides, she was certain that her father would recover and all would be right in the kingdom.

One day she was sitting in the window seat in her father's chamber day dreaming of just this. She imagined doing battle with the dreaded Captain Flint and successfully conveying her father's ships to Orphales and saving the island's inhabitants. Her reverie was interrupted by her father's voice. When she turned around she realized that he must have been awake for some time and had lain in bed staring at her there in the window seat.

"Isa?" his voice sounded stronger than it had in some time "How are you?"

Although his concern was always genuine, something about the way he asked this question troubled her. Attempting to appear cheerful she told him that she was fine and asked how he was feeling.

He looked out the window for a moment before saying, "I'm ready to go there."

"It's awfully cold outside father. It will be better to go out in the spring. We can go for one of our walks then."

He shook his head slowly "I don't mean outside. You know what I mean. I'm ready to leave this, to unwrap." He was gesturing at his body.

She went over and sat on the bed and took his hand. "I'm not ready for you to go yet. I…we need you here. Who will command your fleet? Who will take care of me?"

"Isabelle. I love you more than anything and I don't want to leave you or your mother but you will be alright. I want you to know that you have been the best daughter any man could have ever wished for. You are my darling Isabelle but the time has come."

He moved aside the cover then and she saw the blue morpho. "The time has come to give you what is rightfully yours."

She began to protest to tell him that he would get better but he stopped her. "No. You must have faith that everything will be alright.

Isn't that what you always tell me, to have faith? You have everything you need to carry on."

She wanted so much to be brave but she fell upon him and began to cry. He hugged her tight "I will always love you and I will always be with you. Nothing can stop that. Do you remember what I told you when you were a little girl and we walked on the beach?"

She sniffed back her tears "You told me that you would walk through hell and back for me."

"Yes. I don't want you to ever forget that. I want you to take this box. What you do with it is up to you. Your mother said that you were not ready, you know your mother, but I know that you are."

She told him then how much she loved him and how grateful she was that he was her father. She told him that on some level she knew that she had wished for him as her father when she was still on the other side.

"I wished for you too Isa."

They sat quietly like this for some time until he fell asleep. She was sitting, holding his hand when her mother came in and put her hand on her shoulder. She looked into her mother's face, now a mask of sorrow. The princess stood up, gave her a hug then left the queen with her husband and went to bed.

Isabelle was roused from her sleep just before the crack of dawn. A servant was sent to get her. The Sun Prince had died. She dressed quickly and ran to his chamber. She met her mother at the door who tried to hold her back from the prince's bed but she pushed passed her and ran sobbing to her father's side. She stared into her father's face but she could see that he was gone. She touched his hand and was shocked to discover that it had grown cold so quickly. His great light had gone out and all that remained was a shell. Her mind could not conceive of this. She ran then to her mother who held her as she cried. She could not recall a time before when this had happened and even through her grief she noted how good it felt.

The spell was broken all too soon.

The queen told her, "You are going to have to be strong now. We have much to do to prepare for the state funeral." The queen launched into a litany of what would have to be done.

Isabelle, unable to take it, pushed away from her mother angrily. Her father was dead and her heart was breaking. She did not give a damn about state funerals.

Many Paths, Many Feet

She then ran from the room and down the hall. She did not stop running until she got to the stables. She flung open the door to Philippides' stall, tore off his blanket, grabbed a handful of his black mane and swung her leg over his back. She had no idea where she was going or what she was doing as she set out in the cold blue light of dawn. All she knew was that she had to get away. She gave Philippides a hard kick and gripping tightly to his mane, they tore out of the stable yard. His hoofs echoed on the frozen ground. She crossed the wide front yard headed out of the palace gates and eventually found herself in the forest. She was oblivious to the cold and to the branches that tore her clothes and whipped her face. She pushed her horse on leaving the woods behind. They ran for miles and did not stop until they reached the edge of Crystal Falls.

There she dismounted and was overtaken by the grief that she had attempted to outrun. She turned her face toward the heavens as if looking for an answer there. Tears streamed down her face and she cried, as she had never cried before. She cried until she could cry no more. She found herself huddled at the base of a tree an odd feeling of peace had suddenly washed over her. The forest was so still. The only sound was the water hitting the rocks far beneath her at the foot of the falls. Her eye suddenly caught a movement in the trees. On closer inspection she saw that it was a Peregrine Falcon. She found this strange as she had only seen them before on the edges of the fields. The bird turned its head and looked at her with an almost knowing expression. The young woman and the bird regarded each other for a moment until Isabelle became aware of the cold. Her tears had begun to freeze on her cheeks.

She called for Philippides, mounted him, and turned toward the castle. She walked him, at first slowly then began to trot. She was aware that the falcon was following them, flying from tree to tree and emitting an occasional screech. She felt that the creature was playing with her and she began to ride faster and faster to see if she would follow. As she crossed the final field before reaching the gate Philippides was charging at break-neck speed. Isabelle realized that one misstep now could be deadly but oddly she did not care. She was aware of a growing feeling of joy welling up inside of her. She urged her horse on faster and faster. She was recalling her childhood days, her father by her side, urging her on to the finish line. She could see his loving eyes, his encouraging smile. She knew the falcon was keeping pace with her although she could barely see it out of the corner of her eye.

The sun was rising over the hills now and it had begun to snow. Suddenly a fierce wind kicked up and a small tornado of swirling snow flakes was by her side. She was overtaken by joy and began to laugh as she became aware of her father's presence beside her, racing with her, urging her on. He was playing with her. She was laughing and crying at the same time. The tornado now engulfed her, swirled around her, tickling her, holding her and loving her. She could just make out the palace gate ahead. Her father was challenging her to a race, telling her to go faster and to finish strong as he did when she was a child and he was teaching her foot racing. They were neck and neck. But then as now he was only pretending that she could beat him, that she could run faster than him, but she drove on and with a final kick just made it through the gate before him.

She was laughing hard now and turned to him to say something when just as suddenly as it had come the wind died down. The swirling tornado of snow was no longer beside her. She looked back to see it hovering at the gate for a brief moment then it was gone. She felt the joy recede from her. He would not follow her this time. He had gone as far as he could. She would have to go on alone now.

The next five days were a blur as the household prepared for the funeral. Dignitaries and statesmen came in from all over and many important meetings were held between her mother and her new advisors who had once belonged to the prince. Isabelle spent as much time as she could away from it all, preferring the warmth of the old woman's room.

She sat stoically through the funeral at her mother's side wearing a stiff black dress of paramatta trimmed with crape. She endured long speeches by those who did not even know her father. Her mother did not weep, tears being reserved for private times. The princess was touched, however by those who came up to her later to offer their condolences and to say kind words about her father. After the last of the guests had gone her mother and her advisors retired to her father's study. Isabelle followed.

Apparently the trouble in Orphalese had reached a critical point. They had postponed action for as long as they could. If something was not done soon the colony would be taken over by the buccaneers led by Captain Flint and the inhabitants turned into slaves. Other islands in the region had succumbed to this and the tales were horrifying. With her father's death and the death of his Admiral Gravely there was no one whom the queen trusted to organize their navy and to convey their fleet of merchant vessels to the island.

One of her advisors was in favor of forming an allegiance with a neighboring kingdom that could supply the navy but to enter into this bargain would mean a loss of control of her kingdom and the queen was against this. Another advisor suggested that they cut their losses in Orphalese, rather than shed any more blood but this might signal the end of their burgeoning empire to their enemies and allies alike, and the queen also abhorred this solution.

Half turning toward Isabelle the queen muttered, "If only there was a prince to take your father's place. If I had been blessed to have a son none of this would be happening."

Isabelle knew just want had to be done. "I'll go mother. I will organize the navy and I will re-open the supply lines to Orphalese."

Her mother looked at her daughter as if she had lost her mind. She told her that under no circumstances was she to even consider such a thing and to never mention this preposterous idea again.

Isabelle smoldered with rage "Who then? This is what I was trained for. I was prepared by my father's side. I know what has to be done and what I don't know I will learn."

After some consideration, the queen's advisors suggested that this was a viable solution but the queen would hear none of it. Even with the backing of the advisors and the remaining commander of the navy, Captain Dejois support she refused.

Isabelle and Cythona got into a huge argument, neither of them willing to back down. Isabelle finally stormed from the room. Returning to her own chambers, her mind made up, she tore off her mourning clothes. She would not command the respect of the navy and the other sailors wearing a gown. Grabbing up a large pair of scissors she chopped off her shoulder length hair. She pulled on her black leather breeches and stuffed a few other pair in a bag. She donned a man's shirt and waistcoat over her bodice and grabbed her longest and heaviest coat. All this she tucked into her closet. With or without her mother's blessing she would leave at dawn, but first she must say good bye to her old friend.

It was late but she knew that she would be up waiting for her. Isabelle told her what happened and what she was about to do. The old woman would miss her terribly but she understood that she had to go. Isabelle did not want to leave her either but knew she must. They said a tearful good bye and hugged for a long time. Isabelle promised to write to her as soon as she was able. She was almost down the stairs when she heard it, "Walk good."

When she returned to her room she was shocked to see her mother sitting on her bed.

"What are you doing here mother? If you have come to stop me it won't work. I have the support of those I will command and I am going."

Her mother looked at her wearily and bid her to sit down.

"Isabelle, I have not come to stop you. Of course I don't want you to go but I will not forbid it. I have just lost my husband and I didn't want to lose you too, that's why I tried to stop you, but I understand that you must go. I came to tell you good bye. I will not be seeing you off at dawn because I don't think my heart can take it but I wanted to tell you good bye now and to wish you luck."

Isabelle could not have been more shocked. She stared at her mother for a long moment before throwing her arms about her, bursting into tears. "I don't want to leave you either mother, but I must go. It will be well. Father's spirit will be with me."

The queen held her for a moment then stood to leave "I do love you, you know?"

"I know mother. I love you too."

After her mother had gone she called Xerxes to her and the two of them lay in the middle of the bed to take a nap. She meant to sleep for just a moment but she fell into a deep sleep. She awoke to the sound of tapping on her window and instantly realized that the sun was rising and it was time to go. She went to the window and opened it to find the Peregrine Falcon sitting on the ledge. She put out her arm and the bird jumped onto her fist.

"Well, Xerses. It looks like we have a new member of the family. What shall we name her?"

Xerxes only cocked his head at her (in those days he had not yet learned to speak). "Almitra you say? Alright then Almitra, are you ready for an adventure?"

The bird looked at her with her intelligent eyes. Isabelle took this as a yes, so she finished getting her things together, hoisted Almitra onto her shoulder, and set off for the stables where she ladened Philippides down with her packs (one containing her magic box). She paused at the palace gates to look back at the place where she had grown up. It would be a long time before she would see it again. It was a very cold winter morning as she set off for the port of Abukir. She rode out of the palace gates upon Philippides' back with Almitra on her shoulder and Xerxes at her heels.

Praise

I Have Faith In My Faith

By Verlalia Lewis, MBA

There it is again. Every time I turn on the television, it's the same old story. No jobs, no healthcare, and without those; there is no future. Despite the bad news, I find myself faithfully watching cable and local news broadcasts, at all times of the day and night, waiting to hear some good news. I just needed to hear a "feel good" story to give me a glimmer of hope. Surely there has to be some good news worth reporting. The news reporters were letting me down, but I know exactly where I can go to get the hope I need. I will go to church!

My search for hope led me to attend church service after church service, and I have felt the presence of the Holy Spirit in most of them. But for some reason, the spiritual energy that lifted me so high each Sunday, eventually fizzled out as the week progressed. But I must be totally honest I was not always fully engaged while listening to the sermons. How could I be? The lady sitting on the side of me had on the baddest pair of boots I had ever seen. I wondered where she got them. And then there was the lady sitting in front of me with a rather large green hat that was tipped and laid to the side. And, oh my! I don't remember seeing him here before. He is too handsome! I wonder if he's married. Help me Jesus! There are just too many distractions in these churches. Besides I've heard a lot of these sermons preached by the television evangelists anyway. What was the reason that I got out my nice warm bed? Oh yeah! It was to find some good news.

There must be somewhere I can go that will show me how to make life worth living. Maybe I'll go to the movie theater? Yea, there may be a message in a movie for me.

So, I'll shell out ten bucks for an action packed movie that garnishes my inner strife. Somehow hearing the screams after the gunshots, seeing the blood oozing down the side of the scum bag's mouth and watching the slow downward spiral of an overdose seemed to make me feel much better. Why is that? Is it because, for a few hours, I dissolved my focus from the real "realities" facing me? You know the reality is that some marketing firm is studying my behavioral habits and designing ways to dictate my eating, sleeping and spending habits. Can't I find inspiration anywhere to know that in spite of the viciousness in this world, I can be satisfied? Do I dare desire happiness?

With all of the outer stimulation I was receiving, I felt my inner self being more and more depleted. There was no spiritual or material gain from any of this madness. Weren't all of those contributors outside of myself, (the reporters, the preachers, movie producers, marketing execs) responsible for giving me something to believe in, something that would drive me to want to succeed? Come on, turnabout is fair play, right? I religiously supported them! (Shouldn't their daily goal be to make sure I have what is needed to make my life as meaningful as theirs?) I took this question into my daily meditation and heard the unfortunate answer that I was dreading. It was a resounding NO! I didn't know the "still small voice" could be so loud. "Believe it or not, everything required for you to be successful in this lifetime is within the very heart, mind and soul of you!" WOW, I dropped out of that meditation so fast; I hit my head on the back of the chair! The realization that I had to exhibit successful thoughts, words and actions conjured up fears and paralysis. Exhalation came a few minutes after the room stopped spinning, but GOD made it very clear, no it was crystal clear to me that the ball was in my court. I didn't want to play this game with GOD because I knew he would win. I always let him win and this time would be no different. I have to do this by myself? WOW! Dear Lord, isn't there an easier way out? Wait a minute, I seem to remember another way and it does seem a bit easier. All I have to do is have faith in my cultivated faith!

The doom and gloom stories of the media were coming at me fast and furious and I had to find solid ground to save myself from being swept away in the tide of "economic downturns". Feeling an inclination to shift to a more positive cerebral environment, I began to reprogram the thousands of thoughts in the whirlpool of my mind. I've always tried to be an upbeat and positive kind of person, but there was plenty of room for improvement in this area. Fortunately, the bible verse, "Be ye transformed by the renewing of your mind" was the melody that fueled the whirlpool.

I turned to the self-help sections of many of the popular bookstores to assist in my mind renewal process. I was determined to be a better thinker and to promote a stronger faith in GOD, as well as, in myself. I was relentless in my search and continued to read author after author, after author to assist me in this pilgrimage. The apparent common denominators in all of their writings were the use of the following words: "consciousness", "awareness", "belief" and "faith". These factors are very subtle, yet powerful energies needed to endure the arduous plagues and move the mountains that are necessary to strengthen us. Subsequently, I returned to an inner knowing to seek out my answers.

I say returned because as a child, I learned to trust GOD on a particular occasion that remains with me to this day.

I know that I am a good Christian woman because I got a "head start" thanks to my mother. She read the Bible from cover to cover during the nine months she carried me. Her prayerful state transferred energy to assist me that to this day, I can only explain as the "Holy Spirit" or the grace of GOD guiding me. I am grateful that she had the presence of mind to do that because I have certainly had to draw on that grace many times. It was the strength of that grace that allowed me to incorporate the possibility of something greater (within me and outside of me simultaneously) into my belief system. The opening of that door invited every divine experience I considered necessary to manifest a spiritual path in my young life. The existence of that grace is extremely comforting when I allow its presence to be. My mother's foresight opened up my world to many divine familiarities, including the recognition of Angels through sight and sound that impacted my psyche forever. As a young child, at about age three, I had an "imaginary friend" whom I believed to be an Angel. She had to be; she always showed up when I had fearful emotions or needed something to be explained. But my "sho nuff" (without a shadow of a doubt) awareness of divine activity came when I was 10 years old.

Our family beautician was a very dear friend of my mother's. They attended beauty school together and planned to work side by side in their own beauty shop. Unfortunately, my mother had to release her portion of the dream due to one of the hazards of the job. Back then, to straighten the molecular structure of a Black woman's hair it had to be "pressed". The smoke produced by the hot comb and the pressing grease created an asthmatic condition for her. She couldn't continue to hone her newfound skill, but she wisely chose to continue her beautiful relationship with her newfound friend.

I knew this lady was special from the first time I visited her shop. It didn't seem like the typical beauty shops I'd seen on television. Sure there were pictures of models with various hairstyles, but there were no pictures featuring outlandish colors and hues or "punk do's". But what really got my attention were the scriptures she posted in between the pictures. I distinctly remember one that said, "I must not criticize, condemn or complain, Set a watch before my lips, O' Lord and keep the door to my mouth." Her business was dedicated to GOD and there was no doubt about it. My mother, two sisters, and I were regular customers. We had standing appointments every two weeks. Upon one of my visits, she noticed that my hair was really "broken off" meaning the strands of hair were dry and the ends were jagged and uneven from actual breakage.

It appeared as if my hair was intentionally cut with pinking shears. She had seen this before and knew many factors could contribute to it, but the severity of the damage showed her the root of my problem stemmed from a nervous condition. Intervention was needed and she didn't pass on the opportunity. Delicately, we entered into a conversation in which I was a reluctant participant, but somehow knew my confidences would be respected. After much coaxing, I managed to tell her of my fear of my daddy's volatile temper when he drank. Patiently listening with the ears of her heart, she held my hand and offered her "divine wisdom" to my dilemma. She looked into my eyes and said, "The next time your daddy starts to yell, quietly close your eyes and pray, 'GOD, please help my daddy'." My rapid response fired back as I boldly looked into her eyes and said, "GOD help my daddy? What about, GOD help me?!" I obviously caught her off guard because she pushed out one of those deep down in the belly laughs and then proceeded to explain the scripture, "As you give, so shall you receive." She assured me that sincerely praying for GOD to help my daddy served as a sincere prayer for GOD to help me. Her explanation was very convincing, so I vowed to try it just once. Despite my skepticism, I trusted her enough to stand on these promises of GOD and try this magical spell rendered by the Universe. Just as sure as day crowns the night, the opportunity to test this new theory came to me that very evening. He had been drinking that night before he arrived home and some situation that I don't even remember set my daddy into orbit. I immediately reverted to the tunnel of nervous sweats, shaking and staggered breathing that was so familiar to me during his tirades. Somehow, in the midst of all the chaos that surrounded the moment, I remembered my vow. I closed my eyes and prayed the prayer that would change my life. "GOD please help my daddy, GOD please help my daddy". Over and over, I mentally pushed out the words, so fast and furious that I feared he would audibly hear my silent mantra. I have no idea how much time passed as I stood in that spot praying for the heavens to open up and "beam up" my daddy. But I do know, when I opened my eyes, the magic was in full effect and unfolded right before my very (closed) eyes. My daddy was no longer yelling his head off he was snoring. At some point, he moved to his favorite chair and fell into the deepest, unconscious state that I had ever seen! I was stunned and utterly speechless! I begged my mother to call her friend so that I could give her the wonderful news. When she answered the phone, I excitedly proclaimed, "The magic knocked him out!" My 10-year-old rational mind thought maybe the alcohol kicked in and he had to succumb or that rhythmic tone in the repetition of my mantra was too intense for him. However, my undeveloped spiritual mind knew better. This was the beginning of my creation of faith. I had a sincere desire for a situation to change, while developing the belief in the process. This occasion insisted that I place my faith in something that I knew nothing about so that I could have a greater understanding of what was needed for every situation, every time.

Certain characteristics had to evolve in order for me to excavate the greatness buried so deeply inside me. I had to find and define virtue so that I could make it stick in my life; I had to find value in myself and guard my self-esteem. Who else other than me would be in charge of that? The quickest way to the results I was after was achieved by the utilization of mirroring techniques. It's a very simple process, just "stare" in the mirror, "affirm" the truth while looking into your eyes and "listen" from the depths of your soul. (I named it the look, like, listen technique for short.)

Believe me, I had to look long and hard in the mirror to recognize who I am and face those flaws that chartered my life. I had to re-establish that character in the very fiber of me. I often recited facts like, "Intelligence overflows within me," or "The wisdom of GOD is a vital part of me and I cannot fail". At first, the words were comical to me. When I spoke the words my voice quivered and there was no strength in the volume. I'd laugh very nervously, yet something in the gaze of my stare held my attention and refused to let me make a joke about it. In the intensity of those moments, I could literally see an expansion of energy in my eyes. My pulse and my heart were beating in unison and the cells from the top of my head to the bottom of my feet radiated a wave of "Amen" throughout my body. I was looking into my own pupils, speaking my own truth, vibrating with the cadence of the Universe. For me, this is the peace that passes all understanding and verifies to me that the Father and I are One! I'm not quite sure who should receive the credit for releasing these techniques to our consciousness, but I truly am grateful for their insight! The technique is profound and has much more credibility than I ever realized.

Funny, as a child, I was told to "stop looking in the mirror so much". I now know this was my parent's effort to quash any vain thoughts of beauty that might enter my head. I have fond memories of my daddy telling me, "You've got the nerve to think you're cute," after catching me looking at myself in the bathroom mirror. Well, in my day, girls who "thought they were cute" were frowned upon in school and were often in fights to defend their attitude, so in his defense, I guess my daddy didn't want me to have any altercations. However, had I been allowed to gaze into the mirror, when the desire was there, I feel I would have had a better sense of me and who I was meant to be. After all, it wasn't beauty I was after when I looked into the glass. (Ok, I must confess that I did affirm, "I am beautiful in every way.") I really just needed to see how I was handling the emotions I was feeling. I wanted to see how "fear" had wounded and crippled me or how "joy" was expressed through me! I wasn't trying to be cute; I just wanted a revelation of what kind of person I was becoming. (That's all, daddy.)

As an adult, I simply had to recapture my essence, even if it meant mentally returning to the places that scarred me. So into the looking glass I stared. For hours of days, I stared. My reflection rendered all of the obvious tones that I have features resembling my mother, or when I took a quick glimpse, I saw my older sisters, but that was not all of me. I noticed that as long as I smile, I have distinction, but the minute I stopped, I could see my grandmother's jaw line, which I fondly refer to as those "Mae Anna chops". Wading through the foundations of my facial features, I not only had to "find me" among the sea of relatives, but I also had to "define me". I had to love, honor and respect the "who" that I have become. No one else was stepping forward to give me real instructions on how to do it. Sure I had my support system to say, "You go, girl," but no one was stepping up to show me how to get to the other side of this inferiority that I was harboring. Not even me. This realization hit me like an avalanche. I had to save my own life and I had to do it real quick. I grabbed the psychic scissors and poignantly cut out all of the "poor me" chatter of how I started out with less advantages than everyone else and I didn't stop cutting until I removed every layer of fear and inadequacy. Tears were the antiseptics that healed the layers, as I continued to surge deep into the gut of the matter.

I knew when all of the mindless conversations ceased there would be a void, so I had to think of something positive to fill in the blanks before the hollow rhetoric returned. I reflected back to all of the books that I read and wondered what kinds of thoughts were in the minds of those authors. Did they have access to something that I didn't have? The bottom line was I had to get to the same level of thought or consciousness that they possessed. They had a spiritual truth that I didn't think I had and I so desperately needed to know that truth. Now, I'm fully aware that GOD is no respecter of persons, so the opportunity for me to know this truth, just had to be there for me, too. If I wanted to live a life within "divine parameters" I would have to delve deeper.

So what exactly is "consciousness" and where can I get some? Well, the Merriam Webster Online dictionary defines "consciousness" as "the quality or state of being aware, especially of something within oneself". From that definition, I surmised that if I could allow myself to "believe" there is a substance within me that is all-knowing, then I would be cultivating a "consciousness" and thereby **making it a personal** possession of my own awareness. If I took it a step further and applied a "trust" in that all-knowing substance to direct the path of my actions, I would then develop an absolute "faith" in its guidance. This divine energy is tailor made to my blueprint and will assure that I am in the right place, at the right time, successfully engaged in the right activity! And with daily practice, I will create a confidence in myself because I would be following the guidance designed specifically for me. Oh, this is a big revelation! This knowledge was the key to unlock the cage that fear consistently used to imprison me.

And so the battle to cleanse my mind of those subtle negative thoughts began. It required a concentrated effort because these kinds of thoughts had full reign in my mind on a daily basis. Some of the thoughts were so vile that I even wondered where they came from and how they survived in a supposedly positive vortex. (Surprisingly, I was the epitome of hope and faith among many of my peers). To clear the viciousness, I found myself verbalizing their dismissal with grave authority. "You must leave because I only harbor the Truth and there is no truth in that statement for me" became my mantra to dispose of the garbage flowing within and throughout my mind. My diligence in this process has proven successful in that the words I now speak are tempered with humor, while being concerned for the individual to whom I speak. Through my conscious efforts, the opportunity for healing is made available for both parties in the immediate moment because it is imperative for healing space to thrive whenever and wherever possible. Today my mind is purged of those crippling thoughts and is now abundant with the positive Truth that sets us free!

Though this story highlighting my life is short, the journey that I took was not. There were many times when I felt like giving up because life was too hard and much to my chagrin, I was the one causing the pain by sabotaging my growth in the use of fear, wrong thinking and wrong actions. My thought patterns were developed in the dark, by believing in things outside of myself and by trusting everyone except myself. But now, thank GOD, I have faith in my faith.

I have faith in my decision to listen to the "still small voice within" and trust the direction that is being given to me will produce the highest good for me. And also, for those who inhabit my world. I have unshakable faith in the legion of Angels that are surrounding and protecting us, even if we choose not to acknowledge them. I have faith to know that when I maintain a higher consciousness, or take the higher road, or become the source of light in a situation, I bless everyone in that situation with the freedom to do the same. And because I have unwavering faith, I let my demeanor wax genuine to everyone I meet so they may feel comfortable enough to remember to extend their level of gentility to everyone they meet. Oh yes, faith is the ground on which I stand, and is the foundation on which I create and is the prayer that beckons me to live.

I once was blind, but now I see through the wonderful vision of Faith!

I Prayed

By Phyllis Wilson, MS

I prayed for you today
I prayed for us today
I prayed for help today
I prayed.

I prayed for your love today
I prayed for our spirits today
I prayed for hope today
I prayed.

I prayed for your forgiveness today
I prayed for our love today
I prayed in thanksgiving today
I prayed.

If It Feels This Good Getting Used

By Phyllis Wilson, MS

I woke up excited to attend church as I knew the lessons were always inspirational. I showered and put on a pink and brown silk shantung suit and started to do my hair. As I gazed in the mirror, I could see the multitude of gray sprouting amongst my braids. I must get my hair colored before I have new braids put in I thought. The hair mist made the braids glisten as I tossed the curls to frame my face. I applied my makeup as I always meticulously did and then searched for my strappy brown sandals. I grabbed a cup of coffee and my Bible and headed to church.

Once in the car, I turned on the local gospel station and listened to Yolanda Adams sing "Be Blessed." I smiled and thought, "I AM blessed." I hummed the melody as I merged onto the interstate.

My thoughts then turned to EJ, the love of my life. Last night he came over and we grilled rib-eye steaks and watched a sci-fi movie. I always enjoyed my time with him because he always made me laugh and feel loved. I have been seeing EJ for about three years now and I always hated when our time together would end and he would return home to his wife and four kids. Yes, I was seeing a married man.

I pulled onto the street where the church was located and thought I was early, yet the street was already lined with cars and the parking lot was full. People complained of the parking situation so they tried to get there early to prevent from having to park on another street. I saw an elderly woman wave to me to park in her driveway. I pulled my black Jaguar in and thanked her for letting me park. She said, "No problem, I just want to be a blessing today." She smiled and walked back to her swing on the porch.

As I walked into church, I saw Deacon Barnes and said "Hello, Deacon Barnes."

He replied, "Good morning Sister Harris, it's nice to see you today." I smiled and continued to enter the worship chapel; all the while I knew the deacon was checking me out from the rear. I chuckled to myself.

I eased into one of the back pews as the choir was singing "*Leaning on the Everlasting Arms.*" After a few more selections from the choir, the offering was taken up and the preacher began his sermon. He spoke on repentance from the book of Luke, Chapter 13; "*The door to heaven is narrow. Try hard to enter it. Many people will want to enter there, but they will not be able to get in.*" (Easy Read Version [ERV])

Occasionally my eyes would get heavy but I tried to refocus to help keep from falling asleep. I saw Brother and Sister Johnson sitting in the row in front of me. Brother Johnson was looking intently as the preacher spoke and Sister Johnson looked as mad as hell. They must have had an argument, I thought to myself. Then all of a sudden I saw something out of the corner of my eye, it was white and on my shoulder. I tried to brush it away but it did not disappear. So I turned my head directly to the right and gasped as I saw a little white angel sitting on my shoulder. She smiled and pointed to my left side. I turned my head and to the left I saw a little red devil sitting on my left shoulder waving at me.

I must be hallucinating or asleep I thought. Then the little she-devil said to me, "Why are you here?"

Before I could answer, the angel replied, "Leave her alone!" What?" I replied. Then the she-devil repeated herself. "I am supposed to be here."

Then the she-devil spoke directly to me, "You are a thief, a liar and a cheat. You have not done anything right your entire life. Surely you know that you are going to hell!" I just looked at her. She was no bigger than a thimble yet as fiery as a hot furnace in the wintertime. Spewing devilish words to get my blood pressure up, it was working. I wanted to yell so badly "Shut the H@!! Up!" but I knew I was in church and thought this must be a vivid nightmare.

I turned to the angel and asked her why she wasn't protecting me. She replied, "Just be quiet."

Puzzled I just stared at her as my eyes began to swell with tears. I had no one to protect me from the devil. I was still the same person just cheating and lying to myself about EJ. Although my heart belonged to him, he was married and had been for twenty-three years. He wasn't leaving his family and he made that clear to me from day one, but I let him in. Deep into the crevices of my soul he crept and began to pull the very essence of me into his world. I shut myself off from all my friends and family because they disapproved of him.

"He's just using you," my sister Rochelle said. "He doesn't love you." I snapped in a sing-songy voice, "*Well I wanna' spread the news that if it feels this good getting used... Oh, you just keep on using me, until you use me up, until you use me up*". Rochelle hated when I tried to sing this Bill Wither's song and especially hated this particular refrain.

I knew seeing EJ was wrong. I am no dummy but it was like I was addicted to him and he was my habit. It wasn't just physical, we connected emotionally as well. He knew what I would say before I said anything and likewise. We both liked the same food, music and holding hands. He would hold me if I had a bad day and knew not to say a word as I just wanted to be held. We fit like a hand to a glove and I needed him under his terms. We shared our deepest fears and desires with each other. He even cried in my arms one night as he told me how much he loved and needed me. I truly loved EJ but it is wrong no matter how much you sugar coated it I thought.

The she-devil was right!

Then I heard, *"Get away from me! You are people who do wrong!"* (ERV)

"My salvation is at stake here," I said to myself. "I want to see heaven."

The preacher then began to offer the invitation to the discipleship and people began to walk toward the front of the church. And then it was like I was quietly swept up and carried to the front of the congregation. No more she-devil and no more angels. I approached the preacher and my mouth uttered, "I repent."

The White Envelope
By Quenzette Jackson

"Give and it shall be given unto you; good measure, pressed down, and shaked together, and running over, shall men give unto your bosom. For with the same measure that ye meet with it shall be measured to you again".

—Luke 6:38

One day I prayed to God because I needed a church home. He had given me one in the past, when I lived in Fort Worth with no church home in that city, so I got on my knees and asked for a church home. Lo and behold, when I got off my knees, about five minutes later some ladies walking the neighborhood ministering knocked on my door and invited me to church.

Then about six years ago I prayed again for another church home when I came home to Houston. I went to work the next day and sat at my desk and there, in front of me, was a brochure about a church. I began to read it. Hmm... interesting, I thought to myself, just what I requested. I looked around the room at some of my co-workers desks and did not see another brochure. At the time, I worked for a large company so I looked on top of nearly 15 to 20 desks that day and finally said, "Thank You Jesus" for answering my prayer. Now I had my answer but I still didn't go that Sunday or the next Sunday. Why? Because I was a little frightened. This was a huge church and I didn't know anyone. So a month passed and I walked by my co-worker Bonnye's desk and we started up a conversation about church. And guess what? This was her church. We became great friends. I told her that I wanted to go to her church but was frightened because it was so big. I did accompany her to this church and I joined the second Sunday. I loved the messages presented each Sunday. I felt like I learned more at this church than all my life growing up in church. I was going every Sunday and didn't miss whether rain, sleet or well... there is rarely ever snow in Houston.

At the time my son Marquinn had just left to go into the Navy and was so excited to be traveling that he signed up to serve four years in Japan. I was happy for him but he was my last child at home. I had two children but my daughter Nikkia was already off on her own living her life. I decided to move out of my apartment and help my mom do some repairs on her house. I felt like I was in limbo and it seemed I had nothing to do anymore. I lived with my mom for about six months then moved into my own apartment.

For years I had always dreamed of owning my own house. I said I couldn't wait to get married again so that I could purchase a house with my husband. Bonnye had her own house and didn't feel she had to wait to get married to do so. I said OK God I've been waiting and I know that he is coming because I prayed and I know whatever I ask for I shall receive. I started saving and asked God's help in getting me a house. I also had a little side soap business I ran from my apartment. Bonnye told me that she was going to a trade show and if I wanted she would take some of my soaps with her.

I said "well of course thank you".

The next Sunday at church the pastor asked who's expecting a super natural break through and that's when Bonnye told me she had something for me. I had forgotten all about her selling my soaps for me. She handed me a sealed white envelope with money inside. I didn't have my tithes that Sunday because I had very little left after paying my bills. The pastor proceeded to ask for supernatural debt cancellation in our lives and asked us to give whatever we could. So I took that white envelope, without even looking into it or counting the money, and dropped it into the offering plate. After this I didn't think anything else about it.

At the time, I was driving an SUV that needed some repairs that would cost $850. I didn't have the money to get it fixed. I had to have the truck towed to the apartment and get money from my daughter. She asked me what happened. I was so embarrassed to have to ask for money from my child. I felt as if she should be coming to me.

I went inside my apartment and just broke down crying saying, "I don't care how much I try, things just keep happening. It's like I'm never going to get out of the hole, it keeps getting bigger and bigger."

My daughter said "Don't cry," as she stood there looking at me. I really hated that I broke down in front of her like that because I always wanted her to see how strong mommy was, but I couldn't hold it any longer. Now I realize she needed to see that vulnerable part of me; the part that shows that everyone needs help every now and then and that you just have to ask. All of a sudden I stopped crying and I felt a wave of peace come over me.

I uttered, "I am getting ready to have a breakthrough."

My daughter said, "Huh?" but I said, "I'm okay. I'm getting ready to have a break through."

The next day I got a ride from a co-worker and asked my daughter to come pick me up from work and take me to the dealership to get a car. She agreed and when we arrived at the dealership I saw the car.

I said, "There it is. I want that one."

My daughter protested, "Mom, you haven't even test driven it!"

I thought to myself, I know but something - no it was the Holy Spirit - told me that was the car. I test drove it to settle Nikkia's mind and it drove just wonderfully! We went into the office and filled out the paper work.

The salesman asked, "How much of a down payment do you have?"

I said, "Zero."

He said, "Well, how's your credit?"

"Fair. I'm working on that."

Then he said, "Well let's see who will finance you."

I sat there just as confident that I was going to drive off the lot in a couple of hours in my new car. And what do you know? I did! Five finance companies wanted to finance me. Thank you God!

The next day my realtor called because she hadn't heard from me in about three months, "Ms. Jackson, are you ready to go get that house?"

Again I was confident and I said, "Why yes, if you can find me a brand new house with no money down sure I'm ready."

I called my daughter and asked if she wanted to come with me to see my new house and she said, "Yes mom. What's really going on?"

I said, "I told you that I was getting ready to have a break through!"

I got the car in November for my birthday and I got the brand new house two days after Christmas. It was my Christmas present from God! I gave with my heart all that I had left. I didn't think there was enough in that envelope to bless me with all that he has, but evidently it was. He has blessed me with more than I could imagine.

Jabez Prayer: I Chronicles 4:10
By Rosalee Martin, PhD

I

Jabez prayed from his life of pain
that God would bless him,
not meagerly but abundantly;
Not with wealth alone,
But with a harvest both near and far
of souls who will honor God, his Father.

Jabez,
recognized that his strength came from God,
and *pleaded that God's hands be upon him forever*
so that pain would be a thing of the past;
No longer experienced by him,
and that his life
would be grounded in God's love,
no longer capable of causing pain to others.

And God heard Jabez's earnest prayer,
embraced him by answering it
as soon as it was uttered.

II

Jabez was mentioned only once
in God's Holy Word,
not because of his wealth or power,
Because he had neither. . .
but because he cried to the Lord
out of his pain experienced throughout his life.
He knew that his life could be more than what it was,
But he was not capable of changing it on his own.
He felt trapped by his name;
Living out the prophecy of what his mother called him. . .
Pain;
His name was pain.
He has had his share of it.
But now, his God would break
the yoke given him at birth.

"Bless me indeed," was his utterance;
"Not only for me, but for those my life will touch
both home and abroad. . .so that my past will be
transformed into joy, peace,
love, long-suffering, temperance and kindness,
and that those I meet will be converted by your love
that freely flows through me to them.:
and *God granted him his request.*

III

Jabez was now recognized

For the powerful person he was;

Powerful, not because of his own strength,

For he lived a life of pain;

But powerful because he knew how to connect with God,

to His heavenly Father he cried out, not ashamedly,

but with a belief that his request would be granted.

He cried out for blessings

that only a king could give his son;

Blessings, indeed. . . .

Blessings extensive, ongoing, and in abundance.

Jabez wanted this not only for himself,

but for all those he will meet during his life journey,

knowing that it's God's will

for him to be his brother's keeper.

Jabez knew that blessings alone would not be enough;

But he needed God's hands upon him,

guiding his walk throughout the extended

territory of years, places and resources.

Jabez was a powerful man;

A gift given to him from God. . . .

Not abused, but a good steward;

over all that God gave him.

And we can be powerful too,

following the example of Jabez!

AMEN

Unite

Dear Heart Bandit,

By Sandra Thomas, MA

I'm OK that you took it without asking.

I've even come to grips that you snatched it away when I wasn't looking – how could I fault you when I've grown so accustomed to wearing it on my sleeve?

However, I do implore you—please care for it as if it were your own— in spite of its many imperfections, scars, missing chunks and all.

With time and trials faced together, I hope to view you more than a smooth-talking criminal, rather a compassionate love surgeon intent on restoring this vessel with a renewed capacity for love.

I must admit that on occasion, even under your careful watch, I've noticed it skip several beats and create total catatonic bodily impairment-- of which I feed off like a damsel on life support.

Should you prove to be more than the common thief, my blessing is as follows:

May the one true Healer guide your scalpel ever so gently, and with the fine precision that only you and He possess, extract the years of corrosion and abuse incurred on this vital organ.

Open Letter to My Brothers: BE a Brother
By Phyllis Wilson, MS

Some of you have sisters who mean the world to you and likewise some of us sistas have brothers who mean the world to us. I am talking about the brothers that are our siblings. This open letter is to remind you brothers to LOVE your sisters. Having lost one of my best friends, my brother, almost five years ago to cirrhosis of the liver, there is not a day that goes by that I don't think of him. Yes, he drank a little too much and chased a few women, but all in all he was a GOOD man.

He had such a loving spirit and would do anything for my children and me. He was the UNCLE of all UNCLES. He lived a humble life raisings turkeys and goats in Abilene, Texas, while I lived the fast-paced city life in Houston. He would drive down every holiday to make sure we had everything we needed. When he passed away the town opened up their hearts to me and my family reminiscing about how great a man he was. It was there that I learned that this man, my brother, was loved by a whole lot of people besides me. At his funeral, the church was filled with people of all races, young and old.

He was on disability because he was beginning to lose his memory, yet ironically every time he came for the holidays he made it most memorable. He would bring fresh turkey and eggs each visit. He never cursed me or called me out of my name. He was only a year older than me but he made sure he talked to me about men and the consequences of my choices. He was also famous for his pecan pies. There is not a time that goes by when I see a slice of pecan pie and not want to taste it to see if it was better than his. No one has even come close.

He always encouraged me to 'go for it' and was my personal cheerleader. So if you have a sister out there that is struggling, or even 'doin' just fine' as Mary J. Blige would say, tell her you love her. Encourage her, support her and most importantly pray for her. Love her kids no matter how many different fathers they have and be the UNCLE of all UNCLES.

You see my brother and I were not of the same religious denomination but he reminded me to have the faith of a mustard seed. As I stood at the foot of his hospital bed and his feet were swollen to the size of elephants, I massaged them and begged him to open his eyes because I had a piece of pecan pie for him. He did not move but gasped for air through his oxygen mask. I saw the bag of his urine hanging from the side of the bed half-filled with black fluid. The doctor came in and told me they could not give him a blood transfusion because of his religious beliefs. I cried and screamed and said, "I will take full responsibility for authorizing the blood transfusion," knowing that if he lived my brother may hate me for overriding his decision. But I could not imagine my life without him. As they wheeled him off to X-ray, I heard the nurse shout "Code Blue" and they pushed me out of the room.

As I sat outside his door on the cold ICU floor, I cried and rocked myself and begged God to spare his life. I would give anything. After what seemed eternity, with people rushing in and out his room, the nurse came out and said that he was revived and I could go back in and talk to the doctor. The doctor gave me the forms to sign and said the transfusion would start immediately. As I leaned down to kiss his wrinkled forehead and wipe his face, I whispered, "Nothing will separate us."

He opened his eyes and looked at me and said in a whisper "I will always love you Sis" and slowly closed his eyes. My hands started shaking and I could see he was taking his last breath. The doctor moved me out of the way and said "Code Blue" in a firm voice. Only this time they did not make me leave the room. They announced his death at 2:36 p.m. September 14, 2004.

Now every September I make the journey to Abilene with my now grown kids to see UNCLE Phillip. The ride is always quiet as we are all in deep thought. We clean his gravesite and tell stories about what he has missed since he has been gone. The ride back is always joyful because we think about how he would have reacted if he had known how we have changed. Because of his death my life has been changed forever. I have tried to slow my pace and try to be the AUNT of all AUNTS to my other siblings' kids.

So if you have a sister don't wait too long or till the angels are ready to call you to tell her you love her. Love her now, hug her now, make her smile now, pray for her now, contact her now, support her now, be there for her now, rise up and be the brother she so desperately needs now.

An Independent Woman's Ironic Life

By Ayanna Fears-Betts, BSME

As I sat out on the patio of my oceanfront home in San Diego, I began to fantasize about what it would be like to share my life with someone. I have been so fortunate in my life, a beautiful home, a prestigious career, and all the luxuries one would dream to have. The only missing piece to the puzzle was that special man that I could spend my life with. I thought Gerald would have been "the one", but he just couldn't get past the fact that my career was blossoming and that succeeding in my career was extremely important to me. Why could he not understand that and accept it?

I remember when we first met. He was working in the library of the university we both attended. I was sitting alone reading, and he just boldly walked up to me and asked if I needed a tutor. I was insulted by that and told him straight off! He just laughed and sat down anyway, continuing to talk to me. This bold, confidence was what I found to be the most attractive about him. The fact that he dared to approach me and was not intimidated by my brashness. We dated for eight years and everything seemed to go in the direction of marriage, but the stumbling block to that possibility was Gerald's insistence on trying to change me and make me the "trophy wife". He always tried to convince me that I didn't need to work, that he was going to take care of me. This always started an argument between us. He would often say things to try to confuse and discourage me, too. Like the repeated conversations he started regarding us having children one day and how I could not be a good mother working so many long hours. After having so many of those type conversations, I walked away from that relationship. I did not need it or him.

I definitely want children. Growing up in a single parent home, I feel passionate about the need to have a two-parent environment for children and to be a nurturing mother to my kids. Hell, my Mom left me to my own devices way too many times when I was a child.

I remember a time when my Mom was late coming home from work. I was nine years old and babysitting my younger brother, who was six at the time. She called to tell me to make my brother and me a sandwich to eat until she got home. I remember feeling angry. "Why do I have to always take care of him when she is not here?" I thought to myself. I would rather go outside with my friends and do something fun. My mom would often brag about how mature I was for my age. Actually, she still does when she talks to people about my brother and me. She thinks of me as strong, mature, and self-sufficient. Yeah, I am all of those things, but sometimes I need some help too. Being the oldest child, I had to learn to stay strong, for the sake of my brother, my mom, and my responsibilities.

Now here I am a top-level attorney, with all the things women my age would envy, but all by myself. My dating life in one word: uneventful. Don't get me wrong, I have met some really attractive men, and had some good times, but I am the type of woman who needs more. My friend Lisa is also single. However, she prides herself on meeting wealthy men and getting them to pay her bills and expenses. She believes women have a right to expect the man to pay the way, all the time. She says, if he appreciates what he has, he will have no problem with fronting the bill, the rent, whatever she needs. And the ironic thing is she has had no problem getting men to do it. She admits that she has yet to meet "the one" but just suffices on enjoying her life, as is. I think that is so weak! I recognize that it feels good to have a man want to do things for me, but I also believe that doing for myself keeps me safe. I don't want to be obligated to anyone just because they pay my way. I can take care of my own bills. I don't need anyone to help me. When a man spends money on a woman, there is an expectation established that I just don't want to have to deal with.

My job is the one area of my life that feels right. I am in control of my day and my work. I have overcome a lot of obstacles through my steady climb up the corporate ladder. The men that I have encountered through my career have made me feel like I had to compete. I had to stand on the same level and speak the same language just to earn the same respect. I could not show weakness or sensitivity to gain the respect of my colleagues. I had to be strong and guarded. It was the only way sometimes. I can recall a time early in my career when I was assisting in a defense case and had to go to the state prison with a male colleague to see the defendant. I had never been to a prison facility before and my colleague, Joe, kept teasing me about going to a male prison. I was scared and intimidated, but I couldn't let him know. I kept my cool for the most part but inside I was just praying for the moment we could get the hell out of there. Gotta stay strong, don't let him see you sweat, I kept repeating to myself. I made it through the meeting with my dignity intact, but the experience of having to act like I was so strong, guarded, and unemotional was difficult and frustrating. However, it was then I realized it was a necessary evil for my survival.

Shortly after that experience I realized that I needed to take some time out for myself, but I had so much on my plate and not feeling well was not an excuse I wanted to have to use at work. I was sure I just needed to get some rest and I would start feeling better, but I was experiencing painful headaches that just wouldn't go away.

As I woke up out of a deep sleep, I thought, "Wow, the lighting in this hospital room is bright. And why do they keep it so cold in here?" I didn't even know how many days I was in this hospital, but I knew I would be so glad when I could go home. "Where is that doctor, anyway?" He should be coming in to give me an update on what they found. The only symptoms I had were headaches and a little soreness every now and then. I feel so helpless lying here and weak. I am not used to having no control of my circumstances, waiting on others to tell me my options. Not my style, at all.

"Good Morning, Miss Lewis." "I'm here to take you to get your next set of X-rays."

"Ok," I answered, but in my mind I was thinking, "Oh my god, why did they send this good looking man to get me and I look like hell?!"Excuse me, but can you tell me what day it is and what the doctor has found to be wrong with me?" "No one has told me anything." "Well, the doctor will have to give you the details, but I can tell you that you have been here for a week now." "A week!" "What is wrong with me?" "All I did was go to my doctor about some headaches".

I was so embarrassed to be seen like this, weak and unattractive. I wondered what he was thinking when he looked at me. As he pushed me onto the gurney to go get the X-ray, I tried to look away but I just couldn't help looking at him. And of course, every time I looked up at him he was staring at me. After the X-ray, he brought me back to my room.

He tucked my blankets around me and smiled. "So, when you are not getting X-rays, what do you like to do?"

I thought why is this man asking me such a question? Is he actually interested in me, looking like this? And he has also seen my records and knows that something may be seriously wrong with me.

He said "I'm sorry, if I offended you with that question, I just thought I would lighten up the mood. Also, I just wanted to spend some time talking to you."

"Why?" I asked him. "Don't you see where I am? I look terrible!"

He glanced at me, smiled and said, "I think you are beautiful." "You have been in this same hospital bed for a week in a comma." I realized no one has been here to visit you, so I have been sitting beside you watching you sleep." I knew you would come out of it soon." Why do you care if no one visits me?" "You don't know me." He smiled this smug smile, and said, "I know you don't remember me, but we have met each other before." "You were one of the lawyers defending me 7 years ago when I went to prison for tax evasion."

Remembering Mama

By Lynnell Morrison

Today, when I came home from school
They told me something that was really cruel.
"Go to the hospital, your mother is waiting for you there,"
I didn't understand, but knew this would be hard to bear.

"Go there so your mother can say good-bye."
Why, why, someone please tell me why?
She's in a deep sleep, a coma in fact
I was so confused; I didn't know how to act.

I stood at her bed and called out her name,
She never answered, something was not the same.
My mother is gone, "Where is she?" I said.
I didn't understand as I stood and watched her in bed.

Confused, I left and just walked away
Now I know, I should have stayed.
If only someone had told me so I would understand
I would have stayed and held her hand.

When I got back home, there awaited bad news
I thought, how much more could I lose?
They said after I left, at five fifty-five,
My mother passed and was no longer alive.

She wouldn't just leave me, just up and go,
"Where is she?" I said, I really wanted to know.
I didn't understand, "What's a coma?" I asked.
Tell me so I will know why my mother has passed.

Thinking back two years ago, when I was ten,
And remembering over and over again.
She showed me a large lump on her breast
And since then, I don't think she ever had any rest.

Cancer, this disease, her body, it did infect,
Our futures uncertain, don't know what to expect.
Doctors, hospitals, and surgeries were all to come

I didn't understand, where did this all come from?

I don't know how she did it, with all that life was throwing
Knowing she was ill, no matter what, she just kept going.
My mother, so strong, always a smile and never a frown
She showed me strength and courage, even when she was down.

I didn't know her pain; in private, she cried
I caught her one night; to comfort her, I tried.
Her nights so dark, her days so long
All she would say is nothing is wrong.

I'm just a child, just twelve years old
So tender, too young to watch my life unfold.
"Where is she?" I said, there's no way she's not here
This must be a nightmare; I'm living my worst fear.

As I grow into my teens, oh how I miss my mother
I felt so alone, no one to talk to, no sister, no brother
I had a father and others who helped to look after me
But no one understood that "Mother" was the key.

She was not there to share my precious moments as a teen
Dates, proms, graduation, and more, she should have seen.
I know, if it were possible, she would have been there
Because she had already shown me how much she cared.

I can think of so many things that together we missed
If I started writing, I would never end the list.
As I imagine these things, they make me sad with eyes full of tears
I want her back, I wish I could bring back those years.

I wish she were here, she would have been a grandmother
My two boys will never know their mother's mother.
How could they miss what they never had?
If only they knew, they would be so sad.

Now I know, I can't dwell on what could have been
I must focus now, on spreading her spirit to her living kin.
I can't be sad; I have to be at peace and full of joy,
Strength and courage is what I have to show to my two boys.

I thank God for giving her to me for a short time

She was here long enough to raise me and I turned out just fine.
I know from heaven, everyday, she looks at me
And with a smile, I believe she is pleased.

As I think about it, my boys do have a part of her -
The love from an awesome grandmother.
Through me, she shines as I've raised my boys into fine men.
And today, they are doing the same with their children.

Straight From The Heart

By Lynnell Morrison

How can you say you know how I felt?
When you don't know how many times I've knelt
How many times I've prayed
When I was lonely and afraid

How can you know my struggles?
When you don't know how much I juggle
How much I have been through
When you haven't walked in my shoes

How can you compare my life to yours?
When you don't know that each should be adored
How different each of our paths are
When some are easy and some are hard

Don't feel sorry for me
Whatever has happened was meant to be
And I will show you, so you will see
That God in my life is the key

Regardless of any frustrations
Or any bad situations
Even if my life is a mess
I have always been blessed

What you can do is be my friend

So that my heart can mend

Give me a helping hand

And just say that you understand

Walk beside me and learn my way

Day after day, then you can say

You know how I feel

And straight from the heart, I know you are for real

Mama, Through the Eyes of Her Twelve-Year-Old

By Lynnell Morrison

In 1973, Mama called to me, "Nell, come here, I want to show you something". As I approached her, she proceeded to open her blouse and raise her bra. Showing me her left breast, she said, "I have a lump in my breast." I just stood there, stunned. Even at the age of 10, I knew this was bad. As I looked at her breast, she pointed to a knot and told me that this knot had been there for the past two years and that she thought it was time for her to see a doctor.

Mama went to a doctor and came home and told me, "I have breast cancer. I will have to get my left breast removed." Soon after she had her left breast removed and showed me the end result; nothing but a right breast left. It was awkward for her at first because she had to adjust to "not being complete" and to "still looking good in her clothes". Oh, Mama was a dresser. She liked to be well-dressed at all times, so this was cramping her style, to say the least. Not only is she feeling bad, but now she has to look bad too.

It took a few months, but finally Mama brought home a breast prosthesis from the doctor. From this point on, this is what she wore under her clothes. As long as she wore something with a high neck and the prosthesis didn't move, no one could tell she didn't have two breasts. But, there were problems. It did not stay in place and she constantly had to check herself and re-position her breast prosthesis, her bra, and her clothes. Also, they offered only one color, the color of a Caucasian woman. Mama had brown skin. The contrast was big and she didn't like it.

For awhile Mama felt pretty good as far as her health was concerned, or at least she led me to believe so. But I know better now. As the days, weeks, and months passed, she relied on me more and more to help her. She worked at home as a foster mom and she had a childcare service. There were so many kids in our home on a daily basis; I don't know how she managed, even with my help. I was one of the kids too. Now back then, kids were different than they are today, so she didn't have too many problems out of them. On a daily basis, I went to school, came home and changed my clothes. I then did my homework quickly and went to work at home. I cooked, cleaned, helped with the children, and did whatever else needed to be done. Sometimes, Mama would not need me to help much and I would get to go outside to play. But other times, it seems my chores and responsibilities were endless and I had better not complain about it.

Now there is something you should know. I was adopted. Mama could not have children of her own and I went to live with my parents when I was ten months old and was adopted by my parents when I was two years old. They told me about the adoption when I was five years old and said that I was a "special child" because I was chosen. I believed it. This didn't go over well with the older foster children though. They told me I was not special and for me to stop thinking I was. Since Mama said I was, that is who I listened to and I had no problem telling anyone who I felt needed to know. This is the only conflict I can remember having with the other kids.

It was hard back then understanding why Mama worked me so hard. At the time I felt like she put everything on me. Sometimes she would lie down on the couch while I worked. Now I know she was ill, too ill to do anything physical. Whenever she had energy, she worked hard. Whenever she was physically drained, she still pushed herself until she could go no further. It would be those times she would lie down on the couch. Still while Mama laid down on the couch she would have all of the children surround her. She still kept an eye on them while she tried to rest. Basically, she rested with "the one eye open syndrome".

Over a period of two years, until I was twelve years old, Mama was back and forth to doctor's appointments, specialists, and in and out of the hospital. She was constantly having biopsies and all kinds of tests and treatments. She had more surgeries, including having more cancer removed from her chest. She received blood transfusions. She was exhausted. She would lie down on the couch more and more. She was in a lot of pain.

I would always ask Mama if she was ok, how she was doing, and how she felt. Her answers were always the same, "I'm doing OK" or "I'm fine." She didn't look fine nor did she look OK. I always wondered why she wouldn't just tell me that she was not doing OK. I wanted to help her. I wanted for her to lean on me, to share her hurt with me. She wouldn't. One day while she was lying down on the couch, she was crying. I finally caught her. I asked her, "What is wrong Mama? Why are you crying?" I asked her several times. And her answer every time was, "Nothing is wrong." No matter how much I reached out to her, she would not tell me how she was really doing.

Mama still worked taking care of the children. This was a 24-hour, 7 day a week job, so there were no breaks. She worked even in her sleep. When did she rest? It didn't seem fair. How could she fight cancer when she could not even rest?

As time passed, it became harder and harder for her to keep up with everything that life was throwing at her. The harder she fought this disease the more ill she became. It was very hard to watch Mama at times because she would be in high spirits one minute, but then this disease would pull her in the opposite direction. She would never let anyone of us know that she was having a hard time, that she was scared, or that she was in tremendous pain. She always smiled and listened to her music and acted like nothing was wrong, but if you looked deep into her eyes and soul, you could see the suffering.

Mama had to have a surgery to remove more cancer on January 15, 1975. She needed a blood transfusion. The hospital mistakenly gave her some infected blood and her body could not handle it. She died. She was pronounced dead on five different occasions, each time coming back to life. Finally after a few minutes, she came back to life for the last time. She later told a good friend that she asked God to give her more time; that she had some things that she wanted to take care of first.

For the next two months, Mama was in and out of the hospital more often. She was not herself anymore. She was physically weak. Her pain was unbearable. She had to finally give up some of her children that she cared for during the day. She laid down on that couch most days now. During this period of time, I had no childhood. I basically took over in the care of the children and the chores of the house. I did a lot of the grocery shopping and preparing meals too.

One day, on March 13, 1975, I came home from school and I did not make it into the front door before I was greeted by Mama's friend with, "Come with me to the hospital. Your mother is waiting for you there." I wondered why Mama would be waiting for me at the hospital? This thought boggled my mind during the whole ride there. She had been in and out of the hospital many times now, but never "waited for me" there. *What is going on?* I thought.

When we arrived and began walking towards the hospital, Mama's friend said to me, "Your mother is in a coma." She directed me towards Mama's room and said, "Your mother is in there." I thought to myself, *I could get some answers about what is going on when I see Mama. She will tell me.* I then walked into her room and she laid there on her back with her eyes closed. I stood there for a few minutes, knowing something wasn't right. Then finally, I called out to her, "Mama… Mama…Mama" pausing each time before calling her name again. She never responded. She's never done that to me before. I did not understand what was going on, why did she not wake up? I didn't know what else to do so I walked out of her room. When I walked out Mama's friend said, "Let me take you home." We left so fast I didn't even have a chance to think about going back in Mama's room or asking what a coma was. I sure wish someone would have told me what a coma was because I would have never left. I would have stayed, held Mama's hand, talked to her, kissed her, and told her I loved her.

The ride back home seemed long and was silent. All I could think about was why Mama didn't respond to me. Why would she just lay there and not wake up? I was totally confused. Finally, we were home. There were family and friends at our house along with all the foster children. Everyone was very quiet, which confused me even more.

As soon as we got back home, Daddy and two carloads of family and friends pulled up. Everyone got out of the cars looking sad and everyone was still very quiet. They started hugging me and saying, "I'm sorry." I'm thinking, *Sorry for what?* I am still wondering what is going on and am totally confused about everything.

Then came the news that I never expected, Daddy said that Mama was gone. *Gone where?* I thought. She was just at the hospital lying in the bed. I asked him where she was. He said, "She was pronounced dead at 5:55 p.m. She died right after you left." *That's impossible* I thought. *No way would she leave me and just up and go.* Confused I asked, "What's a coma?" Daddy explained, "It's a deep sleep. Your mother was in a deep sleep and she could not respond to you, but she was still alive. That's why you went to the hospital, so she could say goodbye." I suddenly went from confusion to shock with a little bit of anger. I thought, *Why didn't someone tell me what a coma was BEFORE she died? I was right there at the hospital and blew my very last chance to be with her. I'm just 12 years old. Why wouldn't someone explain this to me?*

For the six days leading up to Mama's funeral, I never cried. I was in shock. Reality had not set in yet. I stayed very busy doing things around the house and helping out in any way that I could. The daycare and extended care parents had come throughout the day and picked up their children. The next day the foster children were picked up, all except for one, a three-year-old boy named Chris.

Why did they let Chris stay but not the others? When they tried to take Chris he kicked and screamed and held on to whatever he could grab. He ran, he fought, he hit, and he would not let go. Chris had been with us for two years. He came to us at the age of one as a very abused and traumatized little boy. He had cigarette burns all over his body from the abuse his mother had inflicted upon him. It took him months to open up to us. When he finally accepted and trusted us, he became very attached to the family, especially to Mama. He took her death harder than anyone. I took care of Chris until the funeral. He grieved for Mama, I did not.

During the funeral, I sat there with everyone watching me and waiting for me to cry. They thought something was wrong with me. I guess that's what shock does to you. I was still numb. I did not cry until I walked up to the casket and saw Mama lying there. It was then that reality hit me. Mama wasn't coming back. She was gone from us forever.

After the funeral life went back to normal. Normal? What was normal? There was nothing normal about my life anymore. My life was turned upside down. I not only lost my mother, I lost my family; all of my "brothers and sisters", except for Chris and my dad. My parents wanted to and had tried to adopt Chris, but were unsuccessful. Had he been adopted he would have been with us forever, instead, he was with us for only six short months.

For the next six months, I cared for Chris after I got home from school, on the weekends, and full time everyday during the three months of summer. Mrs. Moore, a family friend, cared for him while I was in school but she would leave as soon as I got home. Daddy worked until 11 p.m., six days a week, so. I had full responsibility of the household chores and cooking, except for what Mrs. Moore would do while she was there. I didn't mind because I was grieving and that kept me busy. I was accustomed to it because I helped out a lot when Mama was at home sick.

Although I loved caring for Chris, it was a real challenge because of the fact that he was a previously traumatized three year old that was having a very hard time dealing with the death of Mama. He could only express what he was feeling by acting out. He drank bleach. He would go into the refrigerator and eat raw eggs or raw meat. Daddy put locks on all of the cabinets and the refrigerator. Chris would only find something else to do. He spread feces all over the closet door. He would play in the toilet or dump out all of the trash. He would only do these things while Daddy was home. I think that he was afraid he would lose him too and he didn't understand why he was gone all day. He was traumatized all over again.

By the time Chris started to feel better and got more comfortable knowing Daddy and I weren't going anywhere his social worker said that he had enough time with us. He was placed in another foster home. Our home was no longer suitable for him because there was no "mother" figure in the home. Daddy and I visited him about twice a month. After a few months he was then adopted into another family. Talk about devastation to an already traumatized child. Chris did not deserve that, but hopefully a nice, loving family adopted him and it all worked out for him in the end.

As the years went by, it was just Daddy and I. Oh how I missed Mama. It was very hard growing up as a teen without her. She missed all of my special events such as my first date, the senior Mother/Daughter tea, my prom, and graduations. She was not there when I started wearing makeup or got my first boyfriend. She was not there for my high school years. She did not get to meet my friends, and even worse, they did not get to meet her. They did not get to see what a beautiful woman she was and that she was the best mother ever. Where was she at Christmastime; or my birthday when I was blessed with another year? She missed all of those things that she should have been there for.

I felt a sense of abandonment because Mama was gone. I hoped that one day she would come back, but of course she never did. I knew that if she had a choice she would have stayed. Although Daddy grieved just as hard as I did, I felt alone. He wasn't a child, so how could he understand how I felt? I had no sisters, nor any brothers; or anyone who could relate to what I was going through. There were other family members and friends in my life who loved me but somehow there was still someone missing from my life that no one else could replace.

The story continues as I became an adult. Mama would have been so proud of me. In my opinion, she did an awesome job teaching and molding me into the person I am today, however I still wish she were here. She didn't see me go to college, get my first apartment or own my first home. I wish she could have seen how successful my business was. She wasn't there when my children were born. My two sons never knew their grandmother. How could they miss someone they've never known?

Fortunately, Mama's spirit lives in me. She showed me strength and courage. She taught me to never give up. In her eyes, there was no such word as can't or fail. She gave me hope, love, faith, and guidance. She offered me encouragement. She passed on to me her caring, giving, and forgiving nature. She has been my angel in life. She had a heart of gold and she left that for me to hold onto.

And the story continues as my sons become adults. As I raised my boys into men I shared with them Mama's heart of gold. I have given them what she has given me. Now through me, she also lives in them. They turned out to be fine gentlemen. Mama would be so proud.

To my sons, Brandon and Terrence, I love you. Even though you never knew your grandmother, please take her precious heart of gold and hold onto it tight. Use it to live right and to raise your children. Teach them, guide them, and love them. Be strong and courageous. No matter what happens, no matter what life throws at you, never, ever give up. Care about others, give to others, and always forgive others. Always reach high and hope for the best and have faith that it will happen. When your children become adults, you will see that they will turn out just fine. Give them Mama's precious heart of gold, tell them to hold onto it tight, and never let go until they pass it on to their children.

And the story will continue as my grandchildren become adults. They will share their great-grandmother's heart of gold with their children. And Mama will live in them as she will forever live in us.

R.I.P. Ruby Mae Morrison

January 17, 1925 – March 13, 1975

Your job was well done!

Ain't I Human?

By Rosalee Martin, PhD

Why am I loathed,

feared by so many people?

AIN'T I HUMAN?

I have traveled across thousands of miles,

would have preferred to stay home . . .

I hollered, screamed, kicked and tried to run away.

You laughed, tortured me as if

teasing an untamed bull.

AIN'T I HUMAN?

Placed on a ship,

not a luxury liner with men in white coats

to serve our every need . . .

But in a SLAVER -

> lined up

> > back to front;

> > > Sandwiched between my brothers and sisters!

Chain gang!

> pull one

> > ALL MUST MOVE!

AIN'T I HUMAN?

How far from the shore am I?

Can only see darkness . . .

a sea of darkness;

a sea of dark flesh,

> smelling,

> > bruised,

> > > bloody

and wallowing in each other's bodily waste.

Can't see the water or the sky;

except once a day

ten minutes, to be sprinkled with seawater

piercing my cuts,

burning my soul

     etching fear in my mind as I wonder.

AIN'T I HUMAN?

"My God!

     My legs are chained to a dead man . . .

     my brother took the easier way out;

     he willed his death

          knowing that it would be easier than life."

     I dragged him around

          it appears for years . . .

          maybe just hours.

     His body smells

     Maybe it's mine?

AIN'T I HUMAN?

With his mouth twisted, the white demon smirks, shouting,

"another nigger DEAD!

Oh, well!

     MILLIONS!

Should I unchain her from the dead man?

No need to now . . .

     Not much separates the two!

     OVERBOARD he goes!"

A look in his eyes says my time is soon.

AIN'T I HUMAN?

The boat no longer rocks from the angry ocean

that's forced to ingest thousands of Black bodies.

Docks!

>Don't know where;

>Don't know my fate.

Jump to keep the whip from piercing my skin.

Am pulled back by the chain on my ankle.

He jumps under a different beat;

Must coordinate this to move forward and not be whipped.

>**AIN'T I HUMAN?**

Off the ship . . .

step on unfamiliar dry land

looked into a land of whiteness,

piercing me with eyes blue as the sea.

"I hate them already. . ."

The ocean separated me from my motherland;

>from the ones who rocked me in their bosoms;

their eyes looked through me

as if trying to capture my SOUL;

I wrap my arms around my SOUL....

you can do it to my body,

but not my SOUL.

>**AIN'T I HUMAN?**

A hand press against my breast

Prick becomes stiff.

I move from the touch,

anger shoots from his fiery eyes;

his whip cracks in the air.

He was stopped,

"Don't damage the merchandise,

once you buy it, do to it what you will."

AIN'T I HUMAN?

"Sold to the man for $500."

I am carted away with my *new family;*

We don't speak the same language

or come from the same village.

Now we are family;

Must love and trust each other to survive these DEMONS!

Fear grips my body.

"Why live at all?"

I mustn't think that way;

I am stronger than life itself;

I have generations to create;

I have a legacy to leave behind.

I must fight this!

"YOU,

      You wretch,

            move faster when I call you!"

AIN'T I HUMAN?

His hands are all over my body

MY BLACK BODY!

I followed him,

I separated my body from my SOUL!

My BODY is torn open

      He scorns me, but screws me!

      His body jerks inside me;

      His face grimaces;

      He lets out a sigh of pleasure or control or hatred.

      He lies still!

My body aches; my mind is tormented!

I lie still

      Don't want to wake him . . .

Don't want to be beaten by him!

AIN'T I HUMAN?

He moves.

"Get your ass out of here NIGGER!"

I run...

     run back over the ocean;

     run away from the shore;

     run to my country;

     run to my village;

     run into my mother's arms

and scream

     and cry

        and moan . . .

I run to my *new family*;

didn't have to tell them,

they knew . . .

I felt unclean!

AIN'T I HUMAN?

I bore his child, not black like me;

He has poison running in his veins . . .

But out of my body he came;

born of his flesh.

No matter,

     he's still slave like me,

     whipped as others.

No inheritance from rich father who gives

everything to white children.

AIN'T I HUMAN?

Can't throw him away,

though poison run in his veins.

I will suck the poison out;

Love and protect him

from those deadly hands that itch to tear his flesh

and suck his blood till death sneaks in.

I birth him;

he calls me mommy;

he clings to my skirt;

He wants me to hold him.

I birth him and I will teach him

of the warriors of his ancestors;

of royal blood that flows

throughout his motherland.

I will teach him . . .

And he will become a voice

crying in the wilderness.

"Oh, my God!

You can't take my child from me!

My black child!

My only child!"

"You can't . . ."

"Mommy!

Mommy!"

I run towards him . . .

our hands barely touch;

torn away by the devil himself.

Tears. . .

Burning, killing tears

Blur my vision . . .

I won't ever see him again

except through my inner eyes.

AIN'T I HUMAN?

Another child,

  another child,

    another child!

Taken

  Taken

    Taken!

What can I do to keep them?

Cut their toes off;

Maybe fingers . . .

Deform my children

No one wants a deformed child . . .

  But I do!

I get to nurture them, love them,

hold them to my breasts,

grow old together with them . . .

I get to be MOMMY, MOTHER, NANA, GRANDMOTHER!

  AIN'T I HUMAN?

Will it ever end?

Will this violence against me ever end?

Will this violence against my humanity ever end?

Will this violence against my children ever end?

Will my life ever become mine?

I have paid my dues!

My ledger is balanced!

  Against all odds, I gave LIFE to generations . . .

    To mothers, fathers, leaders, doctors, lawyers, teachers,

    inventors, singers, entrepreneurs, dancers, writers,

    engineers, poets, commoners and

  each in their own way will tell my story;

  they will live out my story;

  they will honor my existence!

They will answer my question;

They will say,

> "Blessed is she who birthed generations!
>
> Blessed is she who was
>
> > HUMAN,
> >
> > > And even SUPER human,
> > >
> > > > and even GODLIKE,
> > > >
> > > > > a GODDESS

who will never be forgotten,

and whose legacy will be passed on

from generation to generation."

They will exalt her magnificent life by saying,

"Let **HERSTORY** note. . .

> **YES, SHE IS HUMAN, and in fact**
>
> **the MOTHER OF HUMANITY!"**

Reflect

Wednesday's Child

By Salli Saxton

Monday's child is fair of face,

Tuesday's child is full of grace,

Wednesday's child is full of woe,

Thursday's child has far to go,

Friday's child is loving and giving,

Saturday's child works hard for his living,

And the child that is born on the Sabbath day,

Is bonny and blithe, and good and gay.

-Author Unknown

Many Paths, Many Feet

Chapter 1

It has been said that to be born on a Wednesday is an instant curse. To some, this is a silly superstition, and a wise tale handed down through a nursery rhyme. To me, it is reality. It is my life and it has always been my destiny. As with all curses, there is never a place to run. There is never a place to hide, and although we all may try, you can never change the course of your destiny. I have heard about this curse since the time that I was old enough to understand, and I was around the age of six when my grandmother first revealed my fate to me.

One summer evening while spending summer vacation with my grandmother, she called me outside for a walk with her. It was a walk that we had taken many times together, and it was always a time of peace and contentment for me. Our walks were always taken in the evening, when the night was cool and the stars were just beginning to twinkle. Like a nightly ritual, each walk led us down a trail that ran through a wooded area that lay only a few feet from my grandparent's country home. To this day, I could still walk that trail with perfectly straight steps with my eyes closed, and I can smell the summer jasmine that once bloomed along the path.

On these days, no different than any other, my grandmother would take my hand and we would walk in the cool night air as the stars would shine above us. I can still hear my grandmother's voice, as she would repeat the rhyme "I see the moon, and the moon sees me *God bless the moon and God bless me. For he so loved the world, he gave his son you see. I love God and God loves me.*" I would look far up into the sky and repeat this rhyme with her over and over again. But on this particular evening, as I began to chant the words in a second verse, my grandmother squeezed my hand and silenced my rhyme.

"Anika," she said. "You be a Wednesday's child, destined for a hard life. We did everything we could to stop your mama's labor. But nothing we tried would calm your desire to come into this world one day later or one night earlier. It is not good to be born on a Wednesday. It just ain't good."

I looked into her eyes mixed with trouble and hope, and although I had only a child's concept for what she had just said, I suddenly remembered something that I had overheard somewhere at some time. Without missing a beat, I looked up to her and I quickly said, "But Granny, I'm a big girl and big girl's ain't never afraid to rumble with the devil."

Chapter 2

At 38, I'm still waiting for the devil to show up, and over the years I have even looked forward to it. My motto is "Let's just get it over with, and may the best man stand". I'm ready to rumble and I've prepared myself for the fight. That's not to say that he has kept himself hidden through the years. But the truth, is that he has shown up many times, and always unexpected. The problem is that he has a way of being subtle. He shows up for a time, and then quickly disappears. It's not until after the dust has settled that I even know that he was there. He's a tricky and conniving little demon, and it's because of this, that I hate him even more. A true warrior has no problem showing himself. He's proud of his reputation, and he's ready to prove and show that it's true. But a coward hides behind non-strategic tactics, choosing to pounce only when the unsuspecting victim has his back turned. For this, I have no respect. And for this, I have no fear. But this wisdom is only gained in adulthood. As a child, the devil held me hostage.

There is a condition called phobophobia. It's a real medical condition, and it is defined as having a morbid dread or fear of developing a phobia. Simply put, it's a fear of fear. It's an anxiety condition, which can lead to panic attacks, heart palpitations, shortness of breath, and basically; a paralyzing lifestyle. I once suffered from this condition, and it came over me shortly after realizing what my grandmother actually meant during our walk that summer.

To have someone tell you that your life is destined for doom immediately steals your joy. It takes away all hopes and desires that you may have for your future, and it casts rays of black on any spectrum of color. This is why I never understood why, on God's green earth, anyone would ever pay a palm reader or a psychic just to know their fortune or their future? It's not as beneficial as one may think. Once you've heard the bad news, then just what exactly are you supposed to do about it? We all know that you can't change fate. And if it happens to be good news, then you are always anticipating a day that never seems to come. It's a vicious cycle to fall in, and that's probably how those con artists are able to keep their clientele. Give them the good news first, and then end their session with the bad. This has to be a very effective way to keep a revolving door of paying fools. But, if you were to ask me, I'd tell you not to waste your money. I know firsthand that you can receive your destiny for free.

When I was 10, my phobophobia began to kick in. From that point, I was always looking over my shoulder and waiting for a devastating incident to either take over my life or eventually end it. I never knew for sure what I should fear, but I knew enough to know that I should fear something.

Back in those days, just crossing the street was a source of terror for me. I couldn't even manage to cross the street to get to the elementary school without a panic attack. Even Ms. Karen, the crossing guard could not console or convince me that while she was there, there was never any threat of danger. But to me, her presence didn't matter. No crossing guard in the world could ever stop a car being driven by a curse. Each day I persisted against crossing the street, and each day I held up traffic before Ms. Karen eventually had to drag me to the edge of the sidewalk.

Looking back at those days, I'm sure that this was a sight to see; and for poor Ms. Karen, it had proved to be a constant source of frustration. But, it was one of those situations that I just couldn't help. And at that time, I was just too afraid; too fearful that the moment I stepped my feet onto the pavement to cross; that me *and* Ms. Karen would be hit and left lifeless in the middle of the street.

After about four months of this behavior, Ms. Karen had become more than tired of my performances. At least, that's what *she* called them… *performances.* She had also said that she was tired of me acting like a "damn fool", and that she had planned to call my Aunt Jean and inform her of my ways. In those days, growing up in a small town meant that everyone knew everybody. So it only made sense that not only was Ms. Karen the crossing guard, but she also happened to be good friends with my Aunt Jean. Aunt Jean just happened to be my daddy's sister, and from there, the whole family knew about my embarrassing behavior. From that point on, it was mama who would be the one to drive me to the school and physically walk me into the building. But even with all that, school itself had now proven to be just another source of impending death and a constant trigger for my phobia.

Unlike most kids, my least favorite part of the school day was recess, and I refused to play or participate in any of the games, sports or events. Kickball, tennis, volleyball, or *any* game that needed a ball, or consisted of me having to run *to* or *from* an opponent was out of the question. There were just too many kids running around, too many balls being thrown, too many ways to hurt yourself, and too many ways to die.

During those days of early education, any kid showing signs of stress or a possible mental disorder was quickly put on some kind of mind altering drug to keep them quiet or comatose so that the other "normal" kids could get an education. Back then, it was either forced medical intervention, or to be stuck 20 feet away in that small brick building that was detached from the regular school. This building was the place that held those "other kids". The ones who were disruptive, or who were considered mentally or physically disabled. Whatever their legitimate medical or emotional issues were, they were labeled by most of the kids in my school, (and including most teachers), as being "special" or just plain retarded.

There was that one afternoon when my daddy had been assigned by my mama to pick me up after my last class of the day. Daddy was the first to get off from work during those days, and he was also the parent that commanded the most respect. To act a fool in the presence of my daddy was out of the question, and I knew for me, it would only be another source of an early death. So I had learned early to suppress my fear whenever I was in his presence. I would immediately try to shut down my emotions and fears, even to the point where I would quietly hyperventilate. Any talk of being born on a cursed day would simply not be tolerated. In my daddy's opinion, any day that God gave you was a blessing, and you better act accordingly. In his world, Wednesday's were from the Lord. But to my grandmother, mama, and most of the women on my mama's side of the family, no good ever came of it.

But even in the midst of the devil, God would sometimes show up. Sometimes he would show up in the most peculiar way, or even in the most peculiar people. The only thing about this is that you didn't always notice him right away. He could sit right behind you and you wouldn't even know it. Not until it was time…His time…the right time.

On that particular day, Ms. Price, the guidance counselor showed up after the last class. Ms. Price was a beautiful and tall, dark-skinned black woman. She was always dressed to the nines and she smelled like the jasmine behind my grandparent's home. During those juvenile days, most of the girls in my school idolized her, and most of the boys had secret crushes. But, on this particular day, Ms. Price quietly walked into my classroom, nodded towards me with her signature smile, and pointed for me to come with her. Quickly grabbing my backpack, and happy to be getting out of class a little early, I easily complied. But there was a part of me that wondered why only I had been chosen to leave.

Together we quietly walked outside towards the wooden seating area. Ms. Price would only say that she needed to speak with my parents, but she never elaborated on why. When we finally reached the benches, I began to get nauseated by the smell of her jasmine perfume. The fragrance of jasmine was sometimes a beautiful scent and a beautiful memory, but then there were times when it reminded me of "that day". I tried to redirect my thoughts to keep my stomach calm, but the quiet only accentuated the smell.

Finally, in all that silence, Ms. Price spoke quietly. "Anika," she said first to herself, and then louder to me. "That sure is a pretty name. Does it have meaning?" "Yes ma'am, my mama said that it's Hebrew. It means grace." "Well, that's very appropriate. We all need grace," she said. I twisted in my dress to unwrap it from around my knees. Scooting closer to Ms. Price, I looked up and admired her perfect hair. It was long, straight and black as night. It was at that moment that I made a mental note to myself to never cut my hair. I wanted hair just like that when I grew up...if I grew up. "You know what else?" I said. "What?" she asked with genuine curiosity. "My mama also said that a girl like me would need a lot of God's grace." Ms. Price just smiled, showing her perfect white teeth. "That's right, Anika. We all need it." But I could tell she didn't understand what I meant, and I knew she wouldn't, so I said nothing more.

Again, Ms. Price broke the silence. "Anika, I have a question. Why are you always so sad? You're always to yourself, and sometimes it's like you're afraid of your own shadow." I didn't like her question, and I didn't know how I was supposed to answer that. It's not something most people would understand.

"I don't know. I just don't want to get hurt. I want to keep living," I said. A look of shock crossed her face, and then she turned and looked away from me. Several moments passed when finally, she turned towards me and stared. I always hated when people did that. It was like they could see something in me that I couldn't. A few moments later, the sound of other kids broke my self-consciousness.

Off in the distance, I could see the "special and retarded" kids running from the detached building. Even though the teacher was yelling at them to walk single file, some of them were defiantly disobeying her as if they didn't care that she was in authority. But then there were the others that could not run, even if they wanted to. Those kids had to be wheeled by the teacher or some of the other assistants. I sympathized for those crippled kids. I figured that like me, they must have all been born on a Wednesday too.

But then, there was this one girl that I could not help but notice emerging from the building. She was taller than the other kids, dark as night and she looked just as "special". She also looked mean. That was the first time I had even seen a "special" kid look mean like that. They usually always looked happy. Like they didn't know that there was something wrong with them. I quickly assumed that she must have been one of those problem kids. She was probably one of those students that could never be controlled in class.

I continued to watch the tall black girl. She did not run like some of the others. She obeyed the teacher, but she walked tall, strong and fast. In fact, it looked as if she was walking right towards Ms. Price and me. She had this awful look of betrayal on her face, and I had to quickly think back if I had done something to offend the girl. Maybe I had accidentally ran into her or cut her off in line by accident. I didn't know, and I couldn't think. She was coming too fast and she was looking so mean. I just knew she was going to walk right up to me and punch me in the face. I looked over at Ms. Price and Ms. Price saw her too. She had this look of surprise on her face, and I figured that Ms. Price was the one that must have done something to the girl. It couldn't have been me, I was always too careful. I was always too cautious.

I watched that tall black girl as she kept coming towards us. There was going to be a throw down between the girl and Ms. Price, so I quickly scooted away from her. Even with all the fears that I harbored inside myself, I knew enough to not tempt fate. I could not afford to get caught in that crossfire.

It didn't take long for the tall black girl to reach us. She walked right up to Ms. Price, stopped in her tracks, and then suddenly, her whole expression changed. She had this look of curiosity on her face. Then, without warning, the girl reached out to touch Ms. Price's hair, and then she leaned into her to smell it. At that moment, I knew the girl wasn't normal. She *had* to be one of those "special" kids.

The girl commented on how pretty Ms. Price's hair was and how good it smelled. The girl stood there for a moment and Ms. Price engaged her in a child's conversation. Eventually the girl seemed to get bored with Ms. Price; she turned and looked at me for a moment, and began to quietly hum to herself. She then proceeded to her next destination, which happened to be only a few inches behind Ms. Price and me on the wooden seating bench.

Ms. Price turned her attention back to me. "Anika, what do you mean, you just want to live? What exactly does that mean?" I looked away. Why did we have to be back to that again? Explaining my fate to her would be like explaining God to a group of atheists. Without proof, your belief was meaningless. How could she understand that my birthday was also my death sentence? I knew she just wouldn't get it. "Anika, please tell me. I only want to help you." Ms. Price smiled again with those perfect white teeth, and then, I couldn't help myself.

"I was born on a Wednesday. Everybody knows that it's a curse. Nothing but bad will come to me," I said. Again, there was that long silence, and that look of penetration as if she could see something inside of me that I didn't know was there. I looked off again wishing that I had said nothing. In that quiet moment, I could hear laughter behind us. I turned halfway around, and it was that tall black girl. She was laughing like someone had just told her a funny joke. The only problem was that no one had said anything to her. When she saw me looking, she suddenly stopped. For that moment, she didn't look special anymore. She actually looked much older and much wiser, and she stared at me as if she too saw something that was invisible to me. Again, my self-consciousness returned.

At that same moment, I could hear my daddy's old truck turning down the street. As he approached the building, Ms. Price repeated that she needed to speak to him about me. I watched my daddy do what he always did when he was the one to pick me up from school. He drove right up to the circular drive, opened the passenger side door, and waited for me to get into the truck. But this time, I remained still. Ms. Price stood to approach the truck, she walked up to my daddy's door, leaned in, said something that I could not hear, and motioned for my daddy to park in the parking lot.

It felt like eternity as I watched my daddy park his truck. He stepped his long legs out of the car, and then just stood there for a moment as if he had not planned on dealing with drama today. With wide steps, he reached Ms. Price and me in only a matter of seconds. He looked at me, and then back at Ms. Price as if he already knew what this business was about. Ms. Price extended her hand out to him, offered my daddy her signature smile, and then she motioned that both my daddy and I should follow her into the school.

As we all walked back into the schoolhouse, I turned and looked towards the tall black girl. She caught me looking and she smiled. I couldn't tell if it was a normal smile, or that special smile that kids like her seemed to always have. The one thing I did know for sure was that it wouldn't be long before I joined her in that detached building where they kept those "special" and retarded kids like her.

Chapter 3

The doctor spoke with an odd accent, but the many certificates on the wall gave proof that he was extremely smart and gifted at his profession. He asked to speak to me alone and invited my parents to take a walk around the park that was within clear view of his office window. After my parents left reluctantly, he pointed to a big mahogany chair and told me to have a seat. Once seated, I felt instantly comforted. The chair was huge, but there was something about it that made me feel safe. I looked around the office. This doctor's office was different. It was unlike any other office I had ever been in before, and as soon as I had entered into the office door, I felt instantly transported to Africa.

There was a black table in one corner of the room that had legs like an elephant. On the wall right above the table was a huge picture of women dancers in their African attire. On the floor was a plush zebra rug, and there were many different masks and statues of art on the wall and on the shelves. A wood carving over the door contained the engraved words "WELCOME TO GHANA" The doctor's desk was huge just like the chair that I sat in, and it was the prettiest color of red that I had ever seen. There were various African knick-knacks on his desk, including the wooden penholder, which displayed an engraved name, *Andrew K. Seidu, Psy.D.*

The only thing about this office that was not distinctively African was the classical music that played softly in the background. It was soothing and beautiful and it relaxed me without effort. Because my parents were music lovers and appreciated music of all types, I easily identified the violin as being the main instrument playing throughout the song. For a moment, I began to get lost inside of the music. I watched the doctor as he walked over to the opposite side of his desk, sat in his matching chair and lowered the volume on the remote, which lay next to the engraved penholder and smiled. "Hello Anika, my name is Dr. Seidu" he said, with that odd but soothing accent. "But please call me Andrew." Dr. Andrew was beautiful I thought to myself. He was dark as chocolate, but had teeth white as snow and dimples as deep as the Gulf. It was Ms. Price that had recommended him to my daddy. She said that Dr. Seidu was a child psychologist and that he could be of great benefit to my family and me. She thought that he might be able to help me overcome some of my fears.

At first I was angry about having to see a *shrink*. That's what my cousin Paula had called him after eavesdropping on a conversation between her mother and my daddy. She couldn't wait to come over and tell me that daddy was insisting that he and mama send my crazy behind to a *shrink*. But now, looking at Dr. Seidu, being crazy was a good thing.

"Anika means grace. Did you know that?" Dr. Andrew asked. My eyes lit up and I nodded my head, yes. "God's grace is a beautiful thing, Anika." I was mesmerized by the accent. "It means that God has given you immeasurable favor. It also means to nullify or to do away with. Do you understand this?" I shook my head no. Dr. Andrew leaned back in his chair and smiled another dimpled smile. "Anika, I have talked to Ms.

Price, I have also talked to your father and your mother. I understand that because you were born on a Wednesday, that your mother and grandmother have told you some things about your birthday." I nodded yes. Now, we were off to a good start. "Tell me about it child of grace," he said. "I want to know for myself. In your own words." He leaned in closer and I instantly wanted to tell it all. Even though I was embarrassed, it was good to have someone to listen. For some reason I felt safe with Dr. Andrew and for some reason, I knew he would understand.

"I have to be very careful," I said. The devil will always be on my heels, and if I slip up I can end up in a lot of trouble, or even worse. It's a curse to be born on a Wednesday, it's just not good, and I have to watch my step everywhere I go. There are certain things that I can't do. Some things are normal for most kids, but not for a girl like me. I'm special. I'm different and I have to be careful." I paused for a minute and watched Dr. Andrew's reaction. He winked at me and told me to go on. "People like me can't afford to get caught up in things like others. If I want to live a long life, I have to watch, listen and be careful. That's what Granny says, and so that's what I do."

Dr. Andrew smiled. He seemed delighted with me and I was glad to explain to him my issues with life; and for some reason, it felt good to talk to him. "Anika, you are most definitely right," he said. "You are special because you were born on a Wednesday." Hearing that made me blush and I smiled showing all of my teeth. Finally, someone who understood. He deserved every certificate on that wall.

"And, you know what?" he went on to say. "In my home country of Ghana, Africa we name our children according to the days of the week. It's a traditional ceremony that has been practiced for many, many years." After hearing this, I instantly lit up. "For real? You do that in Ghana?" I asked. "Yep. We sure do. In my country, your name would be Akua, and Ms. Akua, you are most definitely right. You are graced by God. I can see it, I can feel it. The grace that you have from God…that we all get from God is a kindness for which none of us deserve. There is nothing in this world that we have done, or that we can ever do to earn this favor and this gift from God, but yet he gives it to us. God's grace means that you can step wherever you like. You can go wherever you want to go. You can do whatever you want to do. Are you listening to me Akua?" I laughed. I smiled. I definitely liked Dr. Andrew. I nodded my head, yes. "The devil, he is real," he said. "He follows close behind you, but he follows close behind all of us. His mission is ultimate destruction. That's what he does, but the grace that you have been given stops him at every turn. This means that you should have no fear of the devil. No fear of the unknown." Dr. Andrew leaned back in his chair. He threw a dimpled smile, clasped his hands together, and went on. "Listen child of grace, we all have our days, Monday through Sunday, and none of us ever know when bad will happen. Bad can happen to everyone, to anyone, and I will not lie to you. You will have your hard times, but that's life, that's just the way it is. But Akua, it's not a curse. Can you understand this?" Again, I nodded yes, and I truly did understand.

Dr. Andrew stood and walked over to the tall bookcase in the corner of his office. He removed a picture from the top shelf and walked over to my chair. "I have something I want to show you. It is a picture of my daughter. You might even know her because you both go to the same school." He handed the photo to me and I nearly fell out of my chair. It was that tall, black special girl that I had seen a few days before. In her photo, she was holding a violin and smiling like that day was the best day of her life. "I know her." I said. "I have seen her. What is her name?" "Her name is *your* name," he said. "It is Akua. Akua was born on a Wednesday too. Just like you. Akua has some learning difficulties, so she too has had to fight with the devil. Just like you. But Akua works hard and she is a special little girl. She is what we call a musical savant." Hearing this, I was immediately afraid for her. My fears were coming back. "What is that? Is there a cure?" Dr. Andrew laughed, and for some reason, he seemed to truly enjoy my company. "This means that although Akua has some developmental issues, she also displays a remarkable ability to play musical instruments. She has mastered the violin, and is able to play instinctively and without lesson or learning. She has been given a gift from God...just like you. She has been given grace." Dr. Andrew picked up the remote from his desk. He pushed a button, and music began to fill the office. It was the same music that was playing when I first walked in. "That is Akua playing her violin. What do you think of that?" he asked. I said nothing, and I could not help myself. I began to cry. Her music was beautiful. I could not believe that a girl like her was responsible for the melody that filled the office. It was simply moving. Her music and her talent presented a new way of looking at the world, and a new way of looking at myself.

Dr. Andrew smiled and handed me a tissue. "I understand," he said. "Sometimes it makes me cry too." The two of us said nothing during the remaining time of our session. We both just sat and listened to the music. Me in my mahogany chair, and he in his.

Chapter 4

Over the next few years, I spent several more sessions with Dr. Andrew, and I even came to befriend his daughter Akua. In a sense, I came to see Akua as my sister. She had her demons to conquer and so did I. God's grace for Akua was her music and her violin. My saving grace was the caring and sensitivity of Dr. Andrew and the inspiration that I received from Akua.

And now at 38, I can truly say that with age comes wisdom. I no longer look over my shoulder for the devil and he no longer holds me hostage. Just as Dr. Andrew said, and he did not lie, some days are hard, and the devil does his thing. He seeks to bring destruction. But I am always ready to rumble. The grace of God has made me fearless, and the spirit of fear no longer resides inside of me. Forever, I remain a warrior.

In the words of my beloved father, I am Wednesday's child, and Wednesday's are from the Lord.

And So I Leak...

By Tracy René Hayes-Beavers

Sometimes it's just not enough room in here to hold all of me inside. And so I leak...

I walk around masked because to expose the soul that resides within this frame would send many into a head spin and they'd explode with confusion.
...so I leak.

Keep it to myself and I smile and laugh. I silently observe and discuss within my UNSUPERVISED mind the turmoil of humans and relationships and how I fit into it all.
...so I leak.

Feel what I shouldn't for folks that haven't asked me to participate in that part of who they are pretending not to be. However I feel compelled, PUUUUUSHHHHed to seep in under their radar and speak to that confusion in them that also resides in me.
...so I leak.

Want an explanation as to why do we hide who we are, silence what we want, yell obnoxiousness and whisper fears when all we want is to be *loved...*
so I...
Leak sometimes and it's not always because of me.
I leak when I hear my friends distraught over lacking resources.
I leak when I watch my daughter struggle with growing pains.
I leak when I feel my mother missing me over 1,300+ miles away.
I leak when I participate in the joy of a girlfriend finally seeing her dreams come true.
I leak when I feel a man not comfortable with his emerging awareness of his soft side but letting it come out anyway, trusting the process.
I leak when I look at who I am and who I've been and I'm still not really clear on who I want to be.
I leak when the Universe loves me through others and I allow it to penetrate through the mask and lubricate the healing wounds inside my heart.

SO I leak...

because sometimes there's just not enough room in here to hold all of me inside...and that's okay.

I Like...

By Tracy René Hayes-Beavers

I like people who like people.
I like people who like the color orange.
I like people who like baggy blue jeans but not the sagging kind.
I like people who like nice WHITE tennis shoes.
I like people who like chocolate and not hazelnut.
I like people who like to be still…and KNOW.
I like people who like to read books that don't have pictures.
I like people who can write a complete sentence that doesn't use IM abbreviations.
I like people who like animals.
I like people who like little kids (especially the kind you can send home).
I like people who care about life.
I like people who volunteer.
I like people who know a few phrases in more than one language.
I like people who can dance and sing and don't care who's around.
I like people who can step back and observe life occurrences in detached mode.
I like people who aren't intimidated by confidence.
I like people who can speak truth without malice.
I like people who can be honest about what they want and not settle for much less than that.
I like people who believe in fidelity.
I like people who KNOW marriage is NOT about dresses, rings and tuxedos.
I like people who can love hard even when it hurts.
I like people who can cry and laugh about the same situation.
I like people who...like me.

Lest I Forget

By Tracy René Hayes-Beavers

I'm afraid that as I am doing so many other things for someone else I'll forget who I am. So I hold on to bits and pieces of things that I KNOW I like and enjoy because I know that one day soon I'll get a chance to do me. Music, school, languages, singing, dancing, writing…what are my favorite colors again? Funny some people think I'm bohemian. They don't understand that I am a quilt on purpose. I have to maintain something to remind me; so that when I get a chance to be me…I'll have something to start with.

Lest I forget who I be.

I've been a full time mother, wife, provider, life coach, friend, confidante, lover, mistress, side chick, victim, abuser, gofer, *go-to person*, walking library.

I've only been part time to me-- part time to address my needs and concerns in small moments when no one is requesting my presence.

I've done what I heard I was supposed to do. I got married, had children, worked in corporate, had the 401K, tried the college savings, traveled, had benefits, partied and socialized. All the while I maintained my orange, green and white and *a little black*. I held on to my eclectic taste in music even when I was bombarded with hip-hop, rap, blues and zydeco.

I can finish things for others but I don't finish them for myself. I will get to me later…

Lest I forget who I be.

I hold on to the glory of the day I get to begin ME as I define me. Children are growing up and growing on.

Lest I forget who I be.

Raped at 13, I have been spun around and taken off course. Fought hard to hold on to my dreams until they were taken away.

Lost my focus and just merged into the crowd.
Don't wanna draw any attention to myself.
Music was my drug, dancing was my release.
Until he didn't catch me and another dream shattered like my knee on the floor.
Walked away falling deeper into distractions, further off the course.
Trying to sort through faint memories to remember who I wanted to be.
Lost in another distraction, young and facing motherhood, a bad marriage.

Amnesia set in.

The rollercoaster ride was fantastic with highs and lows.
Friends, enemies, a husband, in-laws, who outlawed accepting me.
I'm just holding on until it's my turn. Until others stop asking and needing me to need them and go on about their business so I can do me.

My life is full of pieces like a quilt of interests whose existence is simply to remind me of who I am…

Lest I forget who I be.

So easy to just move from one thing to the next because it's never about me really; doing it for someone else not to get approval or recognition, but because it just needs to get done and what else do I have to do?

Sometimes they stop and ask if I'm okay, If there is anything they can do for me however it's only because they want to pacify me until they are ready to move on to something or someone else.
I've done my best not to get attached to anything so that when it leaves it's okay and I can move on.

I dream about what I wish my life had been like and work it into my "quilt" of me so I can pull it out later when it's my turn…

Lest I forget who I be.

Renaissance of a Peaceful Groove

By Tracy René Hayes-Beavers

I remember the day I woke up, after years of being stuck on stupid and parked on pathetic. I had endured abusive, mentally and emotionally draining relationships, platonic and romantic. I was finally blessed with a healthy, nurturing, spirit-filled union with someone that I'd met in a fast food restaurant. A few words exchanged along with business cards and a promise to call within a month was the jest of our initial encounter.

Weeks later, an email that changed my life…"Is this the phenomenal woman I met in Atlanta?" Late night, early morning phone calls, emails, cards, and letters - we communicated every day, exchanging, feeding one another wisdom gained through life's experiences. Finally, again meeting face to face, and feeling more like old friends than new acquaintances. A peculiar but peaceful familiarity... Love entered. All my adult life had been filled with the labels and the expectations that accompany them which society imposes upon all relationships. I heard… "at least he don't hit you" or "you can't be too picky at your age, divorced with two children." Rarely did I feel God's presence in my relationships except to warn me of danger. I witnessed Love's wings being clipped by impostors to accommodate their insecurities. Co-dependency, self-esteem homicides, vampire-life draining situations with people who were afraid to live, change, grow. I wore the victim mask, playing my part as the martyr, manipulator, naïve Chrissy Snow persona to make them feel better, to avoid being alone. I endured the accumulation of bags of shit that were left as I allowed people to pass through my heart. More like the poop left by puppies called boys trying to be men that I gave myself to when they didn't deserve what I presented to them. We won't even go into the many productions that I co-starred in with the drama queens I tried to befriend. Why is it that females find it necessary to do live autopsies on other female friends only to become jealous, resentful or envious of what they find? Then they proceed to dissect and discredit you for trying to be the best you that you've decided to be just because they haven't arrived at that point yet.

I'd stood within myself…alone, wanting…silent; ready to share and then screaming when they didn't notice or were unable to comprehend my desires. "I'M GIVING YOU WHAT YOU ARE REQUESTING, ALL I ASK IS FOR YOU TO PAY ATTENTION!!!" I yelled as they walked away from me. A spiritual philanthropist I've been dubbed. I'm the one that is understanding, compassionate and always there. I've delayed, swallowed and discarded most of my desires for the peace and happiness of others. I don't regret it. I always seem to receive some type of reward from the Universe but dang, can I get someone to just stop and put me first for a minute?

So I determined that it was me. I was just too dysfunctional to be in a relationship. Silence, isolation and celibacy entered. But this man I'd met in Atlanta, in a fast food restaurant…found me to be amazing from day one. Enchanted with my writing ability, feeling my words, I invited him inside my world. I watched him walk around inside my spirit embracing broken dreams cast in dark corners, dusting off ideas that had been silenced, questioning adventures and ideals not pursued. He gently caressed the cracks in my walls created by internal pressures building for years, dents in the foundation made by abusive words. He inspected the stains of negative entities once present and blew at the cobwebs of my silence through it all. Never judging, instead he was asking…"And what happened here?" He was paying attention.

A vessel through which a strong spirit flowed, he breathed life into the rooms of my world. Guided by THE SPIRIT, an evolving black and just man, whose own spiritual awakening had been misunderstood. Here, he sat in my world as if he had entered some ancient ruin and prepared to study and cherish it's beauty. Introducing his beliefs as they colorfully splashed against the walls of my soul, complimenting the life that was being reborn.

Through our "sessions", I was revived from the emotional coma I'd slipped into after years of unwholesome encounters that had me believing that I was a broken woman, useless to anyone. But God had heard my prayer and sent a man who presented his soul, mind and body for me to embrace and appreciate and I didn't have to crucify myself to get it. Nor did I proceed to attach a label to it. Love is present, guiding us to wherever it sees fit…we are just going for the ride, smelling the sweet blooms of life as we go.

I had finally shed the "Al Bundy" philosophy *what must feel this good will ultimately go sour and it's gonna hurt really bad*, and allowed myself to believe that this piece of peace and happiness was real and really for me. Now understand that I made the mistake of trying to share this experience with those females and males respectively in my life. I spoke about, of course not in detail, how I'd grown as a person and felt so much more at peace with life since meeting this guy. The uniqueness of the experiences we shared. It wasn't just about the physical but how to reach down and be the best me, him, US we could be in the company and trust of each other.

Many Paths, Many Feet

WE even had an agreement that when we no longer brought value to one another's space then it was time to end the relationship…wow! At first, I received compliments that I was radiant, so full of life and excitement, later as I shared more of my relationship, wanting to offer hope and an example for others that it's possible to be happy, the comments changed; I was spending too much time and was seen as "whooped." I was told that long distance relationships do NOT work and I was blind. Surely he was seeing someone else, and I was just too desperate to notice. The bashing began. "Girl you have two kids and he's sooo much younger than you, what do you REALLY think this is about?" I stopped to analyze my relationship, was I missing it again? Had I once again, given myself and all that I am to someone only to be TOO close to see that I was being taken advantage of? I began to sabotage the relationship. You know how we do; start fights, question motives, become negative and insecure. Even his friends questioned our relationship, suggested we needed space to decide if it was real. Still he loved me through my growing frustration and laughed because he KNEW it wasn't me.

It's been over seven years now since we first met. Life successfully killed our romance. Words are powerful and the Universe will answer what you send out. We still talk, still feeding one another wisdom and exchanging experiences, it's different now. We recognize that it is more important to love someone to success than to successfully love them to bed. We focus on developing ourselves in order to contribute to others in our lives. After all, it benefits no one for us to be less than what we have the ability to become. Our conversations are no longer every day, sometimes we go months without a word. We realize that others may find it impossible to be as we are but if we don't…who will. There was a reason we met, a purpose for our crossing one another's path and we may never fully understand. In the meantime, we maintain our friendship… Love is still present…still blooming only seasonally.

WE even had an agreement that when we no longer brought value to one another's space then it was time to end the relationship…

Harlem Is My Home

By Rosalee Martin, PhD

My first memories of life began on 131st Street, between Madison and Fifth Avenue, in the heart of Harlem, in an apartment I was brought to at five days old. Harlem in the 1940s was a black ghetto, with few remnants of its Jewish inception. The old tenant buildings, the symbol of affluence at the turn of the century, were in need of repair. Cracks were in the walls, and the lead in the paint was easily ingested by young occupants, poisoning some and maiming others. The steps were unsafe, their uneven edges cutting into souls that dared to ride their backs ascending into, or descending from the heavens. Despite the hazard of poorly lit halls with rickety steps, thousands of footsteps wobbled up and down those stairs several times a day, oblivious to the danger they held. So much of life was lived in the hallways and on the staircases in those old buildings. The pain of living unfulfilled lives, in a society that devalued their presence, was apparent in the unsteady strides of bent over alcoholics. Holding on the rails as they *fell up* the stairs, these beaten humans spoke of hope for their children, though not for themselves.

Courting occurred in those halls, and the conversations were absorbed by the intrusive walls, which were ever present, but never divulged any secrets. The halls of the five-story building were filled with the chatter of adults and the laughter of children. Up and down we would go from one door to another, picking up a piece of gum here, taking something there, delivering a message to that one, and borrowing some baking powder from the other. There was a system of reciprocity in that building. Sugar given in exchange for babysitting, in exchange for hand-me-down clothes, in exchange for a few dollars, in exchange for cigarettes, in exchange for milk, in exchange for companionship, in exchange for love. Everything had a value and could be used as a commodity at the "market place." The bartering system worked well, reducing the unmet needs of all participants. We were family! We also knew that we better not talk back or be disrespectful to elders because our 'family' had the right to chastise us.

The walls of the apartments housed crowds of people; sometimes two or more families were crammed together like sardines in a space not big enough for a single couple. Many times there were family fights, and the seams of the walls would burst open, violently thrusting some into the hall. Yells of revenge threatened those who dared to cross their paths. Without any place to go, some banged on neighbors' doors, while others cowered under the urine, rat-infested stairwells on the bottom floor. Others became homeless and vacant buildings, condemned for human inhabitants, and were viewed as rent-free penthouses. Without jobs or steady income, selling drugs became a real option. Some joined the army, the best job available for a young Black man. It was wartime and Uncle Sam was gathering as many 'front-liners' as possible, guaranteeing a place to live (in separate barracks), a place to eat (at separate tables), a place to die (buried in separate graveyards). Most Blacks didn't understand that by joining the army they were agreeing to die first. They only saw it as an opportunity. Many of these men left behind families; perhaps one of them fathered one of my brothers or sisters.

There were special people in the building next door to us. That building was better kept than ours. The front door was kept locked, and only those with a key could let themselves in. Each apartment had a bell, which when pressed would open the door for visitors. Some of the people walked with a superiority complex. They felt that they were better than those of us who lived in the other buildings. But I had easy access to that building, anyway. I would go over there several times a week to talk to elderly women who really liked me.

One of them had a front apartment on the ground floor. She was always looking out her window, greeting me every time she saw me. Mommy knew her, and gave me the okay to visit her. It appeared that few people talked to her. There were rumors that she "wasn't all there". I wasn't afraid of her. In fact, I really liked her. She was always nice and kind. Her husband was dead, and she never had any children. I guess I would have been the age of any grandchildren she might have had. We talked about her childhood and how things have *really* changed. I chattered about school and my family. We both enjoyed those visits. She enjoyed them because I listened to her, and I, because I never left there empty handed. She would slip a few pennies in my hands and tell me to go buy something "special for someone special" (referring to me). Now I know that I got more than money for candy from her; from her I got love and a positive sense of self, as well.

Out of her apartment, I would dash down the street about five buildings away. In the basement of the building was a small candy store. That was the favorite place for us kids: big round cookies, two for a penny, 'Mary Jane's' (a peanut butter candy), kitts, and squirrel nuts, were all my favorite treats. "May I have four cookies, two bubble gum, a lollipop, and four squirrel nuts?" I would joyously ask as I laid my ten pennies on the counter. I would leave the store laden with goodies and expecting the popularity they always brought. "No heggies, no bonies, no macaronis," I would say, as all the hands reached out for some of the spoil. Everyone knew just what that meant: "I'm not going to give you any!" So, I would skip down the street, listening to my younger brother and older sisters threaten to tell mommy if I didn't share. Sometimes that worked; most times it didn't. These times I was in control and it felt good.

The cultural outbursts of the Harlem Renaissance had dwindled to a squeak by the time I arrived on the scene. Instead, the streets reeked of odor. The stench of wasted humans on alcohol and drugs was part of my "culture". Kids, out of school, were pitching pennies against the building walls, screaming and hollering as if winning a million dollar lottery. Others were playing cards as if their lives depended on it, ready to cut throat if they believed that someone was cheating.

All types of ball playing could be found on the streets at the same playground where the *Harlem Globetrotters* made their debut. Stickball, dodge ball, basketball, and football were games we played that made us physically strong and fit. We learned how to dodge cars and I can't think of anyone ever getting hit. Mommy and many of the other adults, mainly women, kept watchful eyes on us. They hollered at us to keep out of the streets, threatening to send us upstairs if we didn't, but rarely did they. They quickly forgot their threat as they continued with their own gossip for the day. The men sat around card tables playing spades and dominos. The loud sounds of dominoes hitting the table with, "Let me see you beat this 20 points you M**F**," blended with sounds of children and women on those streets. As a child, I felt secure on those dirty streets of Harlem. There was rarely a boring moment. Talking, fussing, cussing were everyday sounds, interrupted by moments of quiet only a few hours during the night.

The streets were our playground until a real one was built across the street where old brownstone buildings were torn down. We skated up and down the streets, falling and scraping our knees on the rough cement. That didn't stop us. It only increased our determination to succeed. We had no helmets or kneepads or wrist pads to protect us against injury. Our only protection was our skillfulness on skates. Before long we could skate backwards and forward, and did all kinds of tricks. We took such pride in our skills that we would gladly "show-off" to anyone who dared to look our way. I jumped rope, twisting it in circular motions, counting to see how long I could endure.

The greatest skill can be seen when my playmates and I used our ropes to *double-dutch*. A long rope, folded in half was held by two persons on either end. With masterful precision, they would bring one side of the rope over and then the other. In the middle, one, two or three persons would jump so that their feet would not touch the rope. We would jump on one foot, skip, turn around, hop and sing melodies as the rope was moved rhythmically by the two swinging it. We took turns jumping and swinging the rope. I didn't realize that by jumping rope I was developing my large and small motor coordination. I was just having fun! We were just having fun! This rope game is almost extinct today. What a pity!

Little boys made scooters out of wooden crate boxes, using the wheels of skates to make them mobile. Those boxes, discarded as waste by shopkeepers, became treasured possessions. The size of the box inspired the type of car to be made. Bottle tops were nailed at various places on the box to give it a distinctive look. A small can of paint, artistically applied, made those carts on wheels Mercedes and Volvos and Fords. Master builders they were. Those with the "better" carts were respected and could talk some "stuff" to the girls they wanted to impress. They sat their girl on the "two by four" on which the cart was attached while they pushed them, one foot on the board and the other pushing against the concrete. They had so much fun racing each other, and putting each other down while making themselves look good. One time I might be the rider on one of the carts; another day I might be on the sideline, cheering my brother or friends on. Commercial toys were almost non-existent, but no one seemed to notice. Fun was created from the imagination of young minds that worked hard at their play.

As a child my identity was wrapped up into that of my friends and family, and usually I saw myself as a collective "we" instead of "I". Although my sisters and I got along well, I was especially close to my brother, James. We got into a lot of mischief together, and we made a pact that we would not squeal on each other. When we went to the local *Five and Ten Cents* store, we would steal rubber bands and other nonsense things that we did not need. We agreed to let each other curse and never tell. There was a building across the street from us that was gutted out. My elementary school was eventually built there. That building was a gathering place for people of all sorts. It was off limits to us, but James and I would sneak over there and look in amazement at what happened before our eyes: a man and woman partially dressed on top of each other moaning and groaning, some people drinking or using drugs, and other creatively scribbling obscene words on the few remaining walls. Our sex education and education about life began there. James was six and I was eight. As young as he was, James felt responsible for his older sisters. He got into many fights because of us. When he whipped the offender, he felt proud, and so did we. It was good having a brother and sisters.

As brother and sisters, we sometimes fought, but nothing kept us mad at each other for long. We were close in age and in relationship. If Letty, the oldest, said she didn't like something, we would say we didn't like it either. Mommy would tell her to keep her dislikes for food to herself. That way, Mommy would have a better chance to get us to eat certain foods. Usually we mimicked Letty, making it impossible for mommy to force her will on us. I hated green peas. When squashed, the green inside would squirt out, making my skin crawl. To this day, I hate green peas and have never served them to my children.

Mommy, a good seamstress, stretched her money by making us girls our clothes. She would make our dresses alike, and strangers often thought the three of us were triplets. We looked especially sharp on Easter. Mommy would stay up all night sewing on her old machine requiring foot motion to keep it humming and stitching the colorful cloth. The finished product would make clothes sold in *Neiman Marcus* pale in comparison. Patent leather shoes, a bag and a colorful Easter bonnet placed the final touch to our sister act. By the time I was five, even though I was the youngest girl, I was as tall as my two older sisters. Since then I grew faster, and they never caught up with me.

I am sure that every adult on the block played the numbers, i.e. betting on racehorses. You can play the first, middle or the last number or all three numbers. Numbers were played straight or in combination. You get more money if your number came out exactly as you played it. For example, if you played 328 and it came out that way (straight) you get more money than if it came out 238 (combination). The amount you get depends on the amount you placed on it as a $1 play got you less than a $5 play. People played more than one set of numbers, and could spend more than $20 a day. Numbers were obtained from various important dates such as a child's birthday (310 for March 10), or from dreams using a dream book or from newspapers or from intuition (feeling that a number will play) or from any other source. Numbers were written on small pieces of paper, even newspapers and were given to the number man who disappeared until after the numbers came out for that day. Each hoped that it would be the day that their "ship come in". Few conversations between adults ended without some reference to that day's number. Most failed to realize that if they saved the dollars they spent daily on numbers, eventually their dollars would add up to be more than the total of their annual winnings. But playing the numbers was a way of life, and it provided a basis for even strangers to communicate: "Excuse me, did you hear what the 'first' was?" Anyone would know that this question referred to the first of the three numbers that were to come out that day. This initial question was a legitimate way of beginning a conversation with one you had not known previously.

Playing the numbers lined the pocket of white racketeers though we had no contact with them, only the Black runners who got a small 'cut' of the spoils. I knew even back then that whites benefited most by the numbers played by Black people in Harlem. Whites owned organized activities both legal and illegal, and satiated our communities with "opportunities to win". Whites played on the optimism and hope held by Blacks that their "ship will come in". Blacks believed that with their winnings they could move their families out of the ghetto and into the better parts of town. I know that was my mother's hope. She wanted a better life for her four children. She didn't see it happening any other way but by "hitting the number BIG". In addition to losing lots of money, there were other risks associated with playing the numbers, including police busts, and violent acts due to bad deals.

Despite attempts to get rich by hitting the numbers, most women and their children went to church or believed in God. The church provided beliefs, rituals, friendships and a sanctuary from the harshness of life. Mothers prayed that they would hit the number, prayed for the safety of their children, prayed that their welfare check would not be cut off, and prayed about their life circumstances. Church was central to their lives because it was the one place where they were valued as the president of the mission board, deacon of the church, head usher, choir president or director of Sunday school. In the church they had the kind of power that brought respect to them. Respect came regardless of how they lived their lives the rest of the week. In their Sunday best with big-rimmed hats and their Sunday shoes, they were somebody in church and their children were somebody as well. My mother was Methodist and attended a large African Methodist Episcopal Church. I attended that church with her for my early years and participated in many children programs. I remember being in a 'pom-pom mock wedding' where six and seven year olds 'got married'. Girls wore white long dresses with veils, and boys wore a tuxedo. This was a fundraising activity as it brought many saved and sinners to the church to watch their *darlings* get all dressed up. The irony of this activity was that most of the moms were never married themselves.

Mommy made sure that we went to church every Sunday with a few pennies to place in the offering. We would wear the dress that she made and step out in our Sunday patent leather shoes. I sometimes wore bonnets or hats, and of course white gloves to finish my 'Sunday-go-to meeting' wardrobe. The Sunday dress was washed mid-week to be worn the next Sunday. Kids at the church behaved differently from kids on the street. On the streets we were constantly on the move, getting into trouble. But in the church we even held our urine for fear of being accused of playing around. We were more proper as if the Sunday clothes changed our personality; or we knew that if we messed up or disrespected God in His house that our butts would be torn-up when we got home.

But after church, in regular clothes, we would hit the streets and engage in our normal play; and if no adults could hear, would even curse for emphasis.

Pastors, as representatives of God, found fertile ground for yielding power as well; sometimes in non-Christ-like ways. More fundraisers than soul seekers, some ministers had ways to wrestle money from poverty stricken mothers. Money might have come from hitting the numbers or the welfare check. The image of God was a source of contention and contradiction to our blackness, though not always discussed openly. God was a spirit, but his image was white—not at all a reflection of who we were. For many this did not matter, as God the Father brought us out of slavery and saved us from our daily sins. Our beliefs allowed us to look beyond the painted color and to accept His supreme power over our lives as taught by our pastor; at least in theory.

Though we went to church on Sundays and usually Wednesday, many men in our neighborhood went to their 'church' more often. The corner 'beer garden' or bar as we would call it today was frequent by them. My uncle, an alcoholic, would tell us that he was going to church, referring to the bar. He was often 'loaded' or 'feeling good'. The men, full of liquor, with slurred speech would brag about their women, lament about being out of work, moan about their plight in life, and cheery about the prospect of their next drink. Rarely did you hear them talk about us, their children. That was women talk, and because of their inability to support us many ignored us, and in some case, our mothers.

However, a man in my life was my Godfather, the building superintendent, who was around many times a week; but he never lived with us. When I was about eight, he would take my brother and me to storefront churches where he would preach and James and I would sing a duet. He was also a barber with his own shop. We would hang around the shop, listen in on conversations, get pennies from him and the patrons and, of course, go to the store immediately to buy candies. He was about 20 years older than my mother. He befriended her during turbulent times she was having with her aunt, with whom she lived from age 11. Their friendship became more, but his commitment was still to his wife. Mommy's aunt was extremely upset with her for being pregnant for the third time without being married. My Godfather made arrangements for my mother to visit his family in West Virginia so that she could get away from her aunt. She was visiting there when she gave birth to me two weeks prior to her due date.

It was clear that my Godfather loved me, but didn't feel that he could publicly acknowledge me as his daughter because of his marital and religious positions. I was 14 years old when I was told that my Godfather, a married Baptist minister, was my father. When I turned 16 he asked me to change my name to his. He died shortly after that request, and I never gave up my mother's maiden name. I loved my Godfather, as I still call him, and never held resentment against him for not being a full time father to me. He was a constant in my life during my childhood, so that seemed to have been sufficient for me.

My youngest brother, Keith, born when I was eight, was fathered by Mr. Nichols. Although Mr. Nichols lived with us off and on for nine years, he had relationships with other women. He also fathered another child about the same age as Keith These half-brothers lived on the same block, but never acknowledged each other as brothers. Each woman knew of the other, and at times my mother and the other woman 'took to the streets' both verbally and physically. During the times of their conflict, "down the block" became off limits to us. That meant fewer trips to the candy store.

Occasionally, Mr. Nichols would move out, but not for long. It was through him that I had my first contact with the ideology of Marcus Garvey, a Jamaican born leader who came to the United States in 1917 with the hope of creating a strong "Negro" nation in Africa. Mr. Nichols was a strong believer of Garvey's doctrines about Black pride, Black superiority, and Black separatism. He believed, with Garvey, that people of African descent should push for their own state, controlled completely by themselves. It didn't matter which state the United States gave to Blacks, Mr. Nichols would be willing to move to it and establish life there. He felt that only Blacks knew what was good for Blacks, and that whites' input would only dilute Black rule. As a young man Mr. Nichols would attend rallies, and even gave some thought about going back to Africa with Marcus Garvey.

Mr. Nichols was definitely anti-white and anti-religion. He felt that whites used religion to enslave Black people. "Why are you praying to a white God?" Mr. Nichols would say sneeringly. "What has he done for you?" "Besides, Jesus was Black, and not white, contrary to what all of the pictures would indicate," he said quite often. He hung a Black Jesus up in his shop to support his belief. That gesture was certainly before his time. Even now many Blacks have a hard time accepting images of Jesus being Black. What a contrast between his doctrine and that of my mother's, and my Godfather! Mr. Nichols would damn organized religion as an extension of whites' oppression of Blacks. He viewed the Bible as a powerful weapon which kept Blacks enslaved to the ideology of inferiority.

Mr. Nichols, a carpenter, had his shop right down the block over my favorite candy store. Every time I went to get candy, I would go to his shop, unless he and mommy were not speaking at the time. There were always intellectual, heated discussions going on about Garvey's ideology, pros and cons, and the status of Black men and women in America. He never saw himself inferior to anyone, and had no problems voicing his opinion. According to Mr. Nichols, "Black people have to stick together and fight whites if we are to survive as a race." I can see him now, sawing on a piece of wood that he would use in a cabinet he was making, talking about the churchgoers giving their money to the preacher while "the preachers rode around in big cars". He saw preachers and white people as being the same; taking the limited resources of Blacks for their personal gains. I've heard him say this to mommy, who was also a regular churchgoer. Mommy continued to go to church; he continued to curse the church. Their ideological differences didn't interfere with their relationship.

Despite Mr. Nichol's beliefs, there didn't appear to me to be a racial problem, no racial conflicts; just one race, walls and walls of blackness. My neighborhood was all Black; my school was all Black; my teachers were all Black; the shopkeepers where my mother usually shopped were all Black; the church we attended was all Black. I didn't experience discrimination as my encounters with whites were few and far between. I was nine years old, living in the same apartment to which I was brought when I was five days old. I had started school, and loved it from the beginning; I was secure, knowing that caring, watchful eyes were all around me; I played in the streets, went to church on Sundays, played and fought with my siblings. My routine was very comfortable. TV wasn't a household commodity, spreading the venom of white superiority. There were no faces to the voices on the radio. No KKK marched down our streets burning crosses or spreading hatred. My extended family in Charleston, South Carolina experienced that.

Yet, racism was alive and well in Harlem. I was too young to understand the depth of the racial problems, which occurred in Harlem, the extent to which racial groups were isolated and set aside as human waste. As a child, my world consisted of Harlem exclusively. I took only a few bus rides down Madison Avenue where the faces of blackness changed into the faces of whiteness. Along with the changes in facial colors were obvious environmental changes. The ghetto housing and ethnic shops of Harlem changed into exclusive penthouse dwellings and aristocrat shops on Madison Avenue in lower Manhattan. A ride on a single bus weaved you through a colonized community poorly kept by the city, to perfectly manicured communities of power brokers and unimaginable wealth. The two worlds on one avenue reflected the essence of racism; but as a child I didn't know that. Through my child's eyes racism was covert. The daily reminders of forced separate fountains, separate schools, not being allowed to eat at certain restaurants or sleep in hotels were absent from my existence.

I was separate from whites, not because of forced segregation, but because only Blacks lived where I lived. However, even that social fact occurred out of racist actions. The Jews left when Blacks were ushered into Harlem, and relocated in other parts of the city, thus creating de facto segregation. The Jews moved to more desirable parts of the city, closer to the financial heartbeat of Manhattan. And, in many instances they were the financial heartbeat of Manhattan. They moved into places that only people with money could afford, thus recreating a segregated community based upon green power and white power. An invisible wall was created so that Blacks could not move freely in their world, and whites didn't want to move into our world, except to exploit us.

Exploitation existed for us children in a song we sang joyously—'If you you're white you're alright; if you're yellow you're mellow; if you're brown stick around; if you're black get back'. We would sing that song while patting each other's hands, reinforcing subtle internalized racism, though not recognized then. Social, mental and economic pressures placed on Black women like my mother, and Black men like our fathers were also evident and were manifested in occasional self-defeating acts. How often were men and women treated less than human as they tried to secure housing for themselves and their families, employment in order to maintain their independence, education to insure upward mobility, or welfare when all else failed? My mother's state of poverty had racial overtones, with welfare workers trashing our apartment at night in search for a man hidden in her bed, or evidence of material extravagance, like a telephone. These constant pressures may explain some of the criminal activities that occurred in my neighborhood—welfare fraud, thief, violence, drug use, etc. Harlem was a colonized place then; it still is. The new racism has taken the face of gentrification with million-dollar condominiums, an influx of affluent whites with the displacement of poorer Blacks and Hispanics. But when I was a child white faces were rare and none lived in Harlem; only coming to work and leaving to spend their money elsewhere.

Still, my memories of Harlem were more positive than negative and I look back to those days with fondness and some regret. I regret that my life there ended abruptly at age nine. That is another story to be told another time. However, as an adult I returned to Harlem often to visit my mother who relocated there in her later years.

kitten, kat, kougar
By Gloria Scruggs

when I was young, I was old
or so I've been told
but the comments often subconsciously set the tone
in my quest for life, love, and well, lust.

i wasn't committed and often postured that I was the boss
but it came with a stiff cost
that I have yet to define in my head or bed
but I have time, right?

i thought maturity equaled security
and a level of responsibility
but continued to find that the game was the same
wherein the boy with the most toys wins.

i've said all that to say that while I was on my journey
from kitten to kat, I went to sleep
and awakened to find
that now I'm a kougar?

can you help me?
because I thought it was about living, loving and options
that is until I found out my options were no longer
super sized.

i mean what could I do, to widen my pool
    when I was really ole skool?
        with a mantra *"Ain't nutthin' like the love of a brotha!"*
           should I look at others, brothers that is,
             hmmm…

i once laughed when I heard it said,
    "i'm trading in thick and thins,
        for Timberlands"
           at least until I tried it, oooh!

so you see my pool was suddenly widened, to my surprise,
    i mean I was no longer in control, I mean I had no hold
        as I stared into a pair of younger, much fresher eyes.

i must confess, it's a mess,
    a hot mess, and
        oooo weee!

dare I share that there are some younger brothers
    that are not just moving ahead,
        thinking ahead, deeper, committed and ready?
        and oh yeah, did I say deeper?

so if you see me with a young one,
    no he's not my son,
        and I'm happy to report
           that my groove is going,
             on, and on, and on.

Poolside Redemption

By Sandra Thomas, MA

My eyes shot wide open. The sun peaked through the shades, eager to personally introduce me to a new day. This was no ordinary sun salutation, there was an uncanny sense of pride in its greeting; a fortuitous breakthrough from the persistent clouds of gray. Accepting its subtle invitation, I emerged from my ginormous feather and down bed – my heart and head full of a wide range of emotions all competing for first place in the seemingly manic shell I call my skin.

It had been many, many rough months of internal struggle, but the rising sun signaled an impending catharsis. A bittersweet sadness surged through my senses.

This was our last day on the island.

Nearly a year ago, we decided a family vacation was long overdue. (Aside: Hands down I believe I am quite possibly kin to the most erratic, yet fiercely loving family in the universe). To attempt to further describe our unique family dynamic is to digress in an alternate tale, but the three ladies of our nucleus of four decided to venture to *La Isla Encanto*, Puerto Rico for a five-day retreat.

As the days quickly approached for departure I began to realize I did not at all mirror my mom and sister in the budding excitement of the trip to come. If anything, I felt it would be more of a distraction from my preferred pastimes: drowning in my work, meaningless companions, and after hour spirits. The idea of nearly a full week of non-stop interaction with my mother, sister and their two friends (that would join later), weighed heavy on me as I anticipated the chaos, drama, and obligatory conflict to ensue. Too much togetherness does actually exist. I pressed on with feigned enthusiasm and mapped out my first few drinks at the hotel bar.

We landed in San Juan on a fairly muggy afternoon immediately greeted by a throng of beautifully sun-kissed natives. The sweet harmony of Spanglish wafted through the airport and my initial disinterest in this adventure was quickly challenged. I suppose I have always been a creature of comfort and a rebel in the face of change. Since the separation from my ex-husband, I have been hobbling along on feigned pillars of strength, tripping up every once in awhile, not understanding the culprit of my short-term demise. While my self-confidence has taken a major blow over the past very difficult year, I seemed to maintain a modicum of strength, perseverance or most likely, the ability to fake OK.

When it got difficult to fake it, I often attribute my other saving grace to be my family, few close friends and my own fortitude to intangible ideals of strength, courage, independence, self-reliance; everything that would assure I would somehow resurface from the toxic marriage we needlessly endured. At times though, I even caught myself still speaking as "we" when explaining past actions, choices, or decisions made back then. We were not a "we" for a very long time, if ever, but this occasional, (perhaps even Freudian?) slip obliviously revealed the struggle I had in peeling away my own identity from the mess that was. My family's multi-pronged attempt at 'fun in the sun' also hinted at ulterior motives, which was likely their wish for me to step outside of my situation/my life; if only for a few days.

A sense of adventure took over as we waited in the long line of co-vacationers to hail a taxi van to our five-star refuge for the next several days. I began to look forward to a chance to dabble in the art of relaxation: a practice I either lost years ago or never truly acquired. I purchased a recommended bestseller that mirrored my recent life events, toted my laptop to squeeze in some final edits on contract work, and of course plenty of bathing suits.

While I am no avid swimmer, nor does my skin take too kindly to the rays of the melting sun, the mental picture I always retreat to when asked to imagine myself in a serene spot, "my happy place", includes sand, water and bottomless fruity cocktails served by an ever-faithful cabana boy attentive to my every need. I confess; I have an overly active imagination from time to time.

Our taxi dumped us off at the jaw-dropping posh resort so aptly named Lush. The luxurious décor and the friendly nature of the people were instantly contagious. The three of us did not seem to mind the 30-minute wait for check-in as we stood in awe at the sight of our new home away from home for the next several days.

My sister and I shared a room two doors down from my mother and our aunt, who would be arriving shortly. We immediately ran inside and naturally explored in wonder. I had to catch my breath as I opened the double doors leading out onto a huge verandah with the warm sun shining fiercely and the crystal blue expanse of the Atlantic roaring ever so invitingly. The leisurely tourists frolicking in the white sand from a distance looked like speckled little people having the time of their life. There had been relatively few moments in life that I had a chance to cease all physical activity, all restlessness and allow the scene before me to fully set in. The blessings have always been so plentiful whether blinded by whatever current crisis I was to endure. It never fails when I stop to observe it; I am continually moved beyond words.

In the last year prior to this vacation I had been struggling to resolve to be at peace and let go of all the negative emotions that had festered inside of me. There was one emotion in particular that had completely taken a huge chunk of my esteem and slowly eroded my capacity to fully experience joy: Guilt.

I was an adulteress.

In the same vein, marriage to me has always been viewed as the most sacred union. My one long-term personal life goal was to remain in one marriage come hell or high water, accepting my partner and my own flaws and all. My pragmatic personality and wildly unprotected heart certainly had a thing to learn but at the time was convinced Trey and I were meant to last. He was a good Christian man, raised by a good family and who loved me the best he knew how.

Now nearly approaching two and a half years after "I do"; I don't. I actually really could not even fathom, but good 'ol guilt had traded places with my husband.

Snapping back to my present reality I reveled in the visible beauty set before me. "Who's ready for some shots?" I exclaimed. I ran over to my mom's room and ushered her towards the elevator under the guise of a more thorough examination of the glamorous property.

The décor of the hotel looked like the setting of a reality-TV show filmed in some exotic location with modern accoutrements, bright vivid colors, complete with a gorgeous-looking, tan concierge staff with smiles that seemed painted on. From the hotel bar, you could step out onto a deck that wrapped around for what seemed miles while the waves lapped closely against the boulders bordering the property. The palm trees were adorned with wide-swinging hammocks. I staked my claim early on those outdoor beds and let the wind whip through my hair as my eyes feasted on the natural beauty before me.

We asked the bartender to concoct his own specialty libation and floated into the rest of our evening with bursts of excitement for the adventure to come. This was serenity. For now.

For the several days to follow we took part in what I would call exploratory leisure. We spent the first day traveling around by public transport to take in all the city's historical sights. We were the classic tourists soaking in the rich culture, while delighting in the special bond that loved ones create when discovering something new.

Earlier, I made mention of the "erratic" family of mine and so as not to be misleading and represent the vacation as a state of total utopia, I must say we definitely battled our share of conflicting interests, snarky attitudes and general 'too-much-togetherness', but for the most part we gelled in harmony.

On our first full day on the island we decided to visit the historic *Viejo San Juan*. We woke up early, caught brunch at a local restaurant and decided to venture by way of public transportation to the city's oldest barrio; its own small, narrow island off the main land. The weather did not look promising with gray skies and bloated clouds, but we carried on with umbrellas in tow. Our color-coded maps and the fact that most passer-bys spoke both English and Spanish fluently, made this a pretty effortless navigation. We found the free trolley tour, most gratefully hopped aboard and were immediately transported to a moving history class by an animated tour guide who briefly explained the abundant history of the area.

Our guide persisted with his well-practiced script but I tuned out and tuned in to my own understanding of the significance of where exactly we were. This old city was home to a very successful and highly fortified port, with cobblestone streets sharing space with many plazas and colorful Spanish style homes. This bustling port-area and military stronghold began nearly 500 years ago and undoubtedly experienced its share of invasions, natural catastrophes, and threats to its livelihood. But here it remains, intact and distinguished in all its old glory. Even looking around at the people, I noticed a sense of pride in their country and its roots.

What was I gleaning from all of this? The beauty of this city showed me that defeat is acceptance of resignation and that maybe even my limited history marked by its own internal warfare and tear shed is not doomed for future greatness. The road I've been headed down, silently slipping into a state of depression, is a dead end until I opt for acceptance of my past knowing that it ultimately plays a role in my now.

I settled into a somber mood the rest of the afternoon reflecting on the freedoms afforded me now and feeling really ready to close the door to my past once and for all.

The rain fell softly and after several hours of sight seeing, we dodged the drizzle and made our way back to the bus depot. Thankful for the day's lessons, we had a pretty low-key evening with dinner, drinks, and a round of luck at the craps table. I slept well.

My sister, the diligent travel agent, planned an excursion for one-day midway through our trip. We rented a car and drove an hour out into the island to visit El Yunque National Forest. I have never really been one to enjoy spending prolonged time among nature. One year Trey and I went hiking with his family after Thanksgiving dinner. This was when I was still in the mode to pretend for the sake of the in-law bonding ritual and maintain appearances of our happy union. Now what I thought was to be a brisk 10-minute stroll turned into an hour panting, 3-mile upwards trek on a never-ending trail.

However, this time I decided I would shut up, mute complaints and go with the flow. On our drive there, my mom insisted on stopping to eat lunch at a roadside kiosk. To our left was a chain of American fast-food spots, to our right was gravel pavement leading to a dilapidated hut and a pig rotating on a spit. After a pretty bad stomachache from earlier, that was the least desired meal, but *when in Rome...* Needless to say, I picked at the meat and swallowed some rice, tostones (fried plaintains) and beans, quietly dreading the rest of the day ahead.

We took off and reached the rainforest a few hours before the park closed. We first stopped for an information session at the visitor center to learn about the history of El Yunque, then hopped back in the car and began the ascent through the forest.

Breathtaking and serene. My internal whining and sour mood waned. I was awestruck at all the green life surrounding each winding curve.

The sight of the trees and the sound of the animal world immediately transformed me. The magnitude of God's power and creation was the most incredibly humbling feeling I have yet to experience. In the presence of his power and genius, my issues seemed insignificant and laughable.

We pulled over to snap some photos and made our way to La Mina, one of the forest's waterfalls. My sister was the only brave one prepared to fully immerse herself in the downpour, but the rest of us followed for moral support and endured the one-hour hike to La Mina. It was not quite a beginner's hike, but we all pulled together to help my mom and aunt who were falling a bit behind at times. The rain poured heavy on the hike and I did not care one bit. It was warm and flowed all over my body and I could not shake the true feeling of being alive. In the presence of His artistry, I remember swearing to dedicate my life to exploring all of his natural canvases around the world. I remembered this being the high of the trip for me, completely rejuvenating my spirits and reminding me whose I am.

All the lessons each day of the trip did not naturally come full circle to me as I experienced them but, in the days, weeks, and months that followed I was able to connect the pearls of wisdom from each scenario. Its funny the way God intervened and made Himself present in almost all I encountered. Or perhaps, it's funny when I rid myself of life's distractions, that's when I realize He is everywhere, at all times.

The most significant revelation came in the most unsuspecting form and in hindsight can only be understood as one of the most direct - indirect conversations I've had with God.

…This was our last day on the island.

After I threw back the covers and climbed out of the down bed, I realized how difficult leaving would be. It was much worse than any Sunday evening, pre-work week funk. There was a growing knot in my stomach at the thought of leaving the beauty of the island; a place responsible for helping me clear my mind, let my hair down, and lose focus for once from my well-crafted strategies and schedules. This was an unforgettable trip that awakened a desire in me to foster much-needed change in my life.

One of my many inherited traits (from my Mom's side) was the early morning riser gene. My sister and brother can sleep for hours and almost full days, but Mom and I can typically be found up at the crack of dawn, chipper and eager to begin a new day. The night before we talked about how we had spent little time lounging at the pools and planned to begin our morning poolside.

I quietly shuffled through my suitcase as to not wake up my sister, pulled out a new string bikini, grabbed sunscreen, my nearly completed novel and iPod. The excitement for a relaxing morning float out by the pool was starting to eclipse the sadness of the day. Mom and I met up downstairs to grab coffee and started chatting about plans for the afternoon. We got down to the pool, looked around and smiled at each other. We were the only ones with this bright idea. Glorious!

We rented a queen-size float-bed for the day and climbed aboard. With our ear buds and sunglasses in proper place, sunscreen slathered, we were in a whole new happy place. There is something so tranquil about fully relaxing in the company of someone you are so connected with. Sharing a moment like this is often indescribable and although we were both lost in our own private world, the silence between us was beyond comforting.

My mom gets me unlike many people in my life and I've always felt pretty lucky to get to experience her now as both a friend and parent. Through the last difficult year, I feel as if she has really grown to respect me as an adult and understood the decisions I made whether right or wrong, were mine and the beginning of creating a life path made from the meaning we gain from our failures and shortcomings. She knew it had been very tough for me to come to terms with a short-lived marriage and that the punishment Trey and I endured and imposed on each other was slowly deteriorating at both of our senses of worth and capacity to live healthy lives. Mom understood a lot, listened often and said little. That spoke volumes to me.

We floated on in this coma-like state for what felt like hours until we slowly noticed the number of loungers slowly increase. While at first none challenged our acquisition of the entirety of one of the pools, others began to join the waters and we were forced to dodge our new companions. With one eye cocked, I saw a smiling, petite, yellow-boned woman jump in the pool and start to splash around. My immediate territorialism subsided as my desire to pass along the peace to everyone I came in contact with grew.

The woman swam close by and saw our float stuck on the pool's edge. She came over and assisted to launch us off into a different direction. We continued to pass each other every once in awhile and our giant float continued to get stuck due to our lazy steering skills or lack thereof. She offered polite assistance each time and I gave her a big smile. Small talk ensued and we realized we had quite a bit in common. We were relatively in the same age bracket; her approaching her mid 30s and me headed towards mid 20s. She was raised in northern California, while I returned from a six-year stint in So Cal. She had a very warm spirit and our personalities were immediately in sync.

In my line of work, I am often in contact with new people everyday and recently learned I possess a gift of cultivating trust and reflecting a genuine interest in mere strangers. I've realized I intensely feed off these rapid relationships for a truly deeper understanding of the complexities of the human experience.

Sometimes I feel like a sponge eager to absorb any new knowledge about the world and personalities of others' in an overly ambitious attempt at a greater insight into living this so-called life. My expectations are never premature but my keen perception can often call how certain scenarios may play out.

I was unprepared for the conversation with her this day.

My mom realized we were hitting it off and noticed the rest of the gang begin to drift down towards the pool area. She excused herself from the float and offered the space to my new friend—who willingly joined me. After at least a good half hour of get-to-know-you conversation and lots of laughter she abruptly interjected, "Wait hold up. By the way my name is Terry. What's yours?" She extended her hand as we both chuckled realizing we were so engaged and excited about our quick connection we naturally skipped the basics.

"Hi Terry, I'm Sonya. Nice to meet you," I replied.

We quickly reverted back to our lively conversation at hand. She asked me to tell her more about the book I was reading as she heard great things about it. I explained to her it was about a woman in search of herself after a difficult divorce and her travels abroad for a year to fall in love with life and God again. I shared with her how moving the protagonist's tale was and that I envied her courage and strength. In my attempt at being candid and open to the warm soul sharing my float, I told her that I was recently separated and just beginning the process of a divorce.

Terry who seemed to see right through my façade of fortitude called me out on this, "You say this so matter of fact, as if it defines you. Why?" she asked.

Perplexed and pleasantly challenged by her straightforward nature, I decided to further continue rather than dodge the topic. Terry had a unique way of pressing but with a truly empathic tone. It took awhile for me to see that she too had much of the same ability at building relationships with others almost immediately. Her innate sense about my confused state was nailed head on. All I could muster was several attempts at self-analysis, "Well…I don't really know. I suppose it has been a rough year for me and I know I contributed to a lot of the damage that was done. We both did actually. You're right though, I shouldn't let it define who I am."

"Hmm... fair enough" she said. Terry appeared to me as a quiet and watchful listener, I could see her musing on my ambiguity. I could sense her sizing me up, although for what I was unsure.

We sprinkled intimate life facts between surface level understandings of each other's alternate world. Terry was a pastor and pointed across to the other side of the pool and waved at her husband, also a pastor, reading on the chaise lounge. She spoke of their story and how they both shared God's vision and started a church back east.

It's interesting to evaluate the automatic stereotypes we develop when we learn of people's chosen careers and lifestyles. Perhaps in looking back at this chance meeting, I sensed fear in revealing full details of my role in my failing marriage. I often do so because I hide behind a cloak of guilt and shame at my behavior. In this case, particularly opening up to a pastor for further condemnation was not something I felt too open with, at least not at this point in time. She was intent on pushing past the transparent walls I worked hard to maintain at all times. I have always found it extremely difficult to truly open myself up to many people, even those closest in my life. A mere stranger on Sunday morning at the resort pool held no exception.

Terry sensed this and said, "I have not done this with anyone, but I'd like to share my story with you." Caught off guard, but honored that she chose to spend her morning, floating side-by-side in deep conversation with me, I reflected appreciation.

"Sure, of course." I responded carefully.

"Well you see Sonya, I have been where you are. And though you have not told me all the sordid details, I recognize in you a deep struggle you're having in accepting your role in the end of your relationship. I know God has brought us together in this very moment to be a blessing to each other and my hope is that you understand that there is NOTHING he cannot do." I nodded in feigned understanding.

What unfolded from Terry that morning was a story that revealed that even those walking closest to God's side could be led astray and beaten down by the psychological torture Satan best employs. Terry admitted to an extramarital affair for several years with a co-worker at her full-time job. She said that the love relationship between her and her husband after nearly seven years of marriage had grown stale. She often felt misunderstood by him and lacked attention. This man she met at her day job grew to become her best friend. They spent the lunch hour together, laughing and relating and growing a closer bond daily. She grew further apart from her husband and her relationship with God. While Terry had not acted on physical feelings with the other man, she did realize emotionally she had checked out of the marriage.

One day at her job, she and the other man were riding alone on the elevator coming back from lunch. He chose to pull the stop button, which puzzled her, and before she knew it he had physically attacked her and pushed himself against her. She pushed him away and admits that this triggered the beginning of her downward spiral. His advances immediately confused Terry and she no longer viewed him as the patient, caring friend with whom she considered perhaps one day pursuing a true, meaningful relationship. She also learned shortly after that he had dated several women in the office and was particularly known for targeting those that were married. The other man quickly dropped the relationship and Terry was left feeling abandoned, guilty and all alone.

She masked the depression with a growing alcohol addiction. She was never a drinker before but closely following this situation, she began by introducing a glass or two of wine with dinner, then onto vodka and whiskey at night, until finally she was drinking a fifth of vodka in the morning before work in order to endure the unrelenting thoughts of guilt and sadness. She was a walking zombie, so far removed from herself and her faith.

Terry described the couple of months to follow as her quiet downfall. She was able to hide her alcoholism behind claims of feeling ill or retiring to bed early. Her marriage was slipping even further from her reach of repair and she faced demands from her husband to shape up. Looking back she admits being unsure how she managed to keep up appearances for so long. She would still attend church by her husband's side, pastoring and leading their congregation, meanwhile living in her own daily hell.

One day, after several days of calling in sick to work due to her drunken stupors she was summoned to a meeting by her company's Human Resources office, who wanted to discuss her attendance and work performance. Terry's relationship with her boss was very close but her recent slipups and sudden change were red flags that Terry or her boss could no longer ignore. She received probationary status and retreated to her office in a daze.

She said what happened in the moments to follow was nothing short but a cry out to God. She went to the restroom, sat down on the toilet and released what seemed to be all of her insides. She broke down and sobbed and prayed and sobbed some more. This purge signaled her to go home and confess all to her husband and let God take care of the rest. That she did and she began to deal with the demons that had been eating her apart.

Terry said that the reason her husband and her took this trip was because they had finally begun working on the healing process in their marriage. The situation that occurred was a recent event and after months of living separately and beginning the work of repairing the damage they were there on vacation to revive and make whole again what was so close to the end. She admitted her self-defeating thoughts that from time to time rear their ugly head but she mentioned she was a survivor.

"Like I said Sonya, there is NOTHING God cannot do. And each day he takes me by surprise. This chance meeting with you for example is a testimony to that fact. If I had to endure all of that again in order to be a witness and share my story that may uplift and speak to one person, being you, then it was worth it. Our salvation is always worth it."

At this point, tears were pouring down my cheeks as I listened to all her wisdom and truly understood for the first time our humanity. The understanding that God took my affair along with the multitude of other acts I've committed and will commit and allowed His whole and perfect son to cover was and at times still remains unfathomable. The fact that I had for so long been unable to receive His grace was also. Instead, I've chosen to live this past year in limbo, feeling unworthy of forgiveness from anyone, resigned to a life of broken relationships, and constantly feeling low.

Terry and I grabbed each other's hand and she asked if she could pray over me. Her words, which were not her own, convicted me so strongly and resounded loudly in my soul. It was then I realized it was beyond time for me to let it go. Get on with living and release my self-imposed bondage.

There is something so naturally healing about sharing your story to someone so far removed from the cause and effect. All too often we find ourselves in our heads spinning irrational thoughts like a DJ on the 1s and 2s. We constantly find ourselves shuffling through the details that hang us up. We get stuck replaying the anger, the guilt, and all the things that hinder us from moving past the roadblocks on the path to healing.

It was only God intervening that very morning compelling Terry and I to gravitate towards each other on the super float and collide our stories to impact each other in one of the greatest ways. He had been trying so very hard in the last year to demonstrate to the both of us his boundless mercy and grace.

Terry left me with some deep soul searching, reintroducing me to my unconditional Father. In the midst of the pain, "Count it All Joy" she said.

Author Profiles

Many Paths, Many Feet

Tracy René Hayes-Beavers

Tracy René Hayes-Beavers is a native of Cleveland, OH who now resides in Houston, TX with her son Ryan and daughter, Colbe. A gifted writer with several web-published works, Tracy combines her careers in writing and community mental health. She is a dynamic motivational speaker who is adept at building bridges across members of diverse groups and promoting team cohesiveness through structured and informal learning opportunities.

She co-founded the strategic consulting firm, Ibis International that provides training and publication guidance to individuals, non-profit and corporate clientele. Through Ibis, Tracy has been instrumental in developing teen discussion groups at middle and high schools; facilitating workshops for parents; and establishing tools for self-esteem, personal actualization and stress management. Tracy has been a member of the Tavis Smiley Foundation National Advisory Committee since 2004, where she offers her unique perspective in co-creating curriculum and workshop content for over 200 youth leaders.

With a passion for women to "know thy self", Tracy established SELF DNA with the support of a psychologist and co-facilitated a weekly holistic group for women of color.. As an avid volunteer with recognitions ranging from most Outstanding Texan Volunteer by Texas Congressman Al Green, to the first African American Moxy Woman by International Association of Moxy Women in 2007, Tracy continues to dedicate her time to coaching young people and women on relationships and personal growth.

Many Paths, Many Feet includes excerpts from Tracy's upcoming publication, <u>Journey to a Peaceful Groove</u>; a bio-journal that combines her poetry, blogs and personal correspondence to chronicle life lessons.

Many Paths, Many Feet

Ayanna Fears-Betts, BSME

Ayanna Fears-Betts, BSME, comes from a background in engineering design, manufacturing, and operations. She has over 13 years of professional experience in several different industries. She started her professional career while still attending college in her junior year at the University of Louisville in Louisville, KY. She began working as a Production Supervisor for a cigarette manufacturing company during the time when the cigarette industry received a lot of negative press in the media.

Being a woman of color, and younger than the average supervisor or manager in her field has always played a part in Ayanna's identification. She hopes to provide a voice to women in her similar background.

Ayanna is currently working as an Operations Plant Manager for a food manufacturing company and is a member of the American Society of Mechanical Engineers (ASME). She is also the proud mother of two teenage children and enjoys spending time with family and friends.

Ayanna may be contacted at:

Meengineer123@hotmail.com

Many Paths, Many Feet

Dr. Nicole Cutts

Nicole Cutts, Ph.D., licensed Clinical Psychologist, Success Coach, Artist and Organizational Consultant has for over 10 years been inspiring and empowering people to achieve a more balanced and successful lifestyle. Through her companies Cutts Consulting, LLC and Vision Quest Retreats, Dr. Cutts has coached and trained leaders and teams at Fortune 500 Companies, Federal Government Agencies, and Non-Profit Organizations. As a master facilitator and Success Coach, she helps people create an exceptional life by honoring their mind, body, and spirit so they can experience joy, passion, meaning, and ultimate success in their work.

Dr. Cutts is a featured writer on the Walter Kaitz Foundation website and has been a contributing writer for *Identity Television, Black Chambers Online*, and *The Diversity Channel,* where she was also the Senior Features Editor. She has been featured on BET, the BBC, Black Enterprise Magazine, and various radio programs. She has co-authored and published several articles in scientific and literary journals. Her writings on Corporate Wellness, Success Coaching, and Diversity have appeared on several Chamber of Commerce and business websites. She is a former faculty member in the Women's Studies Department at The University of Maryland-Baltimore County.

She received her Ph.D. from the California School of Professional Psychology – LA and her B.S. in Psychology from Howard University.

She is currently collecting stories for a book in progress about women living their visions of success. To contribute visit her blog, *The Vision Quest Chronicles* at www.cuttsconsulting.com/wp/

Nicole may be contacted at:

Cutts Consulting, LLC and Vision Quest Retreats
Dr.cutts@cuttsconsulting.com
www.visionquestretreats.com

Quenzette Jackson

Quenzette Jackson, a native Houstonian, can often be found crafting and designing speciality soaps for her home-based business, Soapgram. The proud mother of two delivers a narrative through her adventurous personality about her life experiences that continue to help her grow spiritually and mentally everyday. Ever since Quenzette was a little girl she's had a great passion for books and writing. Many times she put her love for writing aside because of children, education, and her career, but when the opportunity finally presented itself she took on the challenge with developing her first published short story.

Quenzette may be contacted at:

quenzettejackson@gmail.com
or quen2711@swbell.net

Paula Jemison, MA

P aula Jemison is a senior executive communicator with nearly 15 years of experience in the area of corporate communications specializing in strategic global public affairs. She has been highly successful in leading cost-effective internal and external communications, crisis and issues management and media relations campaigns for global oil and gas companies. As a former journalist covering local news in Florida and state politics in Illinois, Paula has had the opportunity to interview leaders in the community and prominent political figures, such as Rev. Jesse Jackson and former US Senator and presidential candidate Bob Dole.

Paula has a Master's of Art in Public Affairs Reporting with an emphasis on state politics and governmental relations and a Bachelor's of Art in Broadcast Journalism and a minor in Marketing. She is also a fellow of the Poynter Institute of Media Studies.

She knows no strangers. Her goal in life is to inspire and touch as many lives as she can through community involvement and writing. She is currently working on her first novel, which she hopes to publish soon. She has three children and resides in Houston.

Paula is available for full-time or contract work, facilitating workshops, event planning, media training or wherever there's a need for a highly effective communicator.

Paula may be contacted at:

paulaj@manypathsmanyfeet.com

Verlalia Lewis, MBA

Verlalia Lewis is a spiritual advisor, public servant, massage therapist, reflexologist and philanthropist. Born in Kansas City, MO, she graduated from Center Senior High School and continued her education at Prairie View A&M University in Prairie View, TX where she majored in Home Economics and minored in Business Administration. She has a MBA in International Business from Our Lady of the Lake University in San Antonio, TX.

However, her greatest satisfaction in life comes from her self-appointment as a "Good Will Ambassador" for peace and spiritual authenticity. It is important enough to her to motivate any and everyone to aspire to a higher consciousness, so as to experience a fuller life.

"Whether you choose your successes to be grand or small, the Universe is willing to create them all!"

Verlalia may be contacted at:
vlewis@manypathsmanyfeet.com

Dr. Rosalee R. Martin

Rosalee Martin, PhD and native New Yorker, has a Master of Science in Social Work and a PhD in Sociology. Additionally, she is a Licensed Professional Counselor, Licensed Master Social Worker and Licensed Chemical Dependency Counselor. Dr. Martin currently teaches at Huston-Tillotson University in Austin, Texas where she has been a master teacher for more than 38 years. As a private consultant and therapist, Dr. Martin specializes in the areas of Conflict Resolution, Cultural Diversity, Violence, Self-Esteem, HIV/AID, Sexuality, Parenting and Addictions. Additionally, Dr. Martin provides prevention education to churches and other community organizations, locally and abroad.

Dr. Martin is a published author of a variety of professional works related to her areas of specialization, children's books, and pamphlets. She was a weekly contributing author to two grassroots newspapers in the area of drugs, sex and AIDS and other health related issues. She is a self-published poet and has seven chat books. She was recognized for her literary works in 1984 and 1994 when she received an *Outstanding Authors Award* from Delta Sigma Theta Sorority, Inc.

In her leisure time, she enjoys her children, grandchildren, reading, writing, photography and missionary work. She has also traveled extensively to five African nations, Caribbean, Central America, Europe and South America.

Dr. Martin may be contacted at:

Rosemar3@hotmail.com

Lynnell R. Morrison

Lynnell R. Morrison has 30 years of business experience. Experimenting since childhood, after taking an entrepreneurial class in school, she first began by trading services and products for money. She soon learned that she had a unique talent in this area and became a professional entrepreneur. Being a single mother, she also noticed that good quality childcare was hard to come by. Combining her business skills with a lifetime of experience in childcare and a need to be there for her own children, she started a licensed childcare business in Los Angeles, California. Her goal was to give young children the best start in life possible, all while providing a dependable place where parents could bring their children and not have to worry about how their child was doing. They had no doubt that their child was doing great.

Lynnell has recently made her home in Houston, Texas, where she continues to use her entrepreneurial skills. Outside of her business life, her children and grandchildren are the love of her life. She loves to spend time with family and friends, as well as travel whenever the opportunity permits.

Lynnell may be contacted at:

(337) 263-6060
LynnellMorrison@manypathsmanyfeet.com

Salli Y. Saxton

Salli Y. Saxton started writing as a young adult. Her "inner author" was set free one evening when a woman in her social group proposed that everyone had a book inside of them. This revelation provided the perfect inspiration for her to write her first short story, WEDNESDAY'S CHILD.

Currently, an Administrative Assistant in the largest medical center in the world, she lives in Houston, TX with her son Joshua. In addition to writing short stories in her spare times, she is learning web design, loves to read, travel and enjoys the simple pleasures of life.

Many Paths, Many Feet

Gloria Scruggs

Gloria Scruggs has experience in corporate public relations, corporate, board and community fund development and giving and relationships, program planning and development, fund raising, strategic planning, management and training, special event planning, and customer service. She holds a bachelor of science from the University of Michigan-Flint in health care administration and human behavior and has participated in many professional development seminars and workshops throughout her career. She has held progressively increasing positions in the health care, business and legal fields and is passionate about helping others.

If you're out in the community of Greater Flint, Michigan, you may run into Gloria Scruggs utilizing her diverse skills in various community endeavors. Serving on the board of directors of the Foundation for Mott Community College, Genesee County Community Mental Health, University of Michigan-Flint School of Health Professions and Studies, and the Urban League of Flint has given her a professional outlet, as well as an opportunity to serve others.

Gloria's selection *kitten, kat, kougar* is a little break from her professional persona and relates to humorous discussions with friends about an amusing aspect of growing older and relationships.

Gloria may be contacted at:

gloscruggs@manypathsmanyfeet.com

Many Paths, Many Feet

Lynn Simpson, MBA

Lynn Simpson was born and raised in New Jersey until relocating to Austin, TX in 2008. She is the owner and founder of Lotus Blossom Events and Wedding Planning. Lynn has more than fifteen years of event planning and business development with various companies and non-profits. Lynn is currently a business instructor for a four year college, she also volunteers with many community organizations and serves as a mentor to youths and young adults, and Executive Director of a woman's networking organization. In addition, she has created an Investment Club called the Women's Wealth Society. With undergraduate degrees in Business and Education, Lynn has played an integral role in educating the unemployed and underemployed of her community on ways to overcome some of life's obstacles.

Lynn also holds a Bachelor of Science from Rider University, Lawrenceville, NJ and a Master's Degree in Business Administration with a minor in Marketing from American Intercontinental University.

She shares her message of "Manual NOT Included" to help youth and young adults understand that the decisions they make today can effect their tomorrow. Her ability to reach out to the masses and understand the decisions they have before them allows her to connect with her audience and answer the questions from "their" perspectives.

Lynn may be contacted at:

lynnsimpson@manypathsmanyfeet.com

Lotus Blossom Event & Wedding Planning
www.LotusBlossomEvents.com
Lynn@LotusBlossomEvents.info

Many Paths, Many Feet

Sandra Thomas, MA

Sandra Thomas comes from a human services background with several years experience in service-related roles. Her background includes non-profit marketing & development, health administration and neuropsychological assessments. Sandra is dedicated to cultivating her expertise in the area of personal growth and development for individuals and organizations committed to the community and social justice issues.

Sandra is an alumna of Pepperdine University where she received her undergraduate degrees in Intercultural Communications and Psychology. She furthered her vocational pursuits and attended Pepperdine University's Graduate School of Education and Psychology earning her Master's Degree in Psychology.

With a heart for children and youth, Sandra is currently pursuing licensure as a Licensed Specialist in School Psychology at the University of Houston-Clear Lake and Board Certification as a Licensed Psychological Associate in the state of Texas.

In her spare time, Sandra enjoys exploring the vastness of Houston, reading, traveling, escaping to museums, and working on interior design & do-it-yourself projects. Sandra is also available for marketing and consulting projects, project management and publication editing.

Sandra may be contacted at:

3am Strategies & Consulting
(310) 266-6364
sthomas@3amstrategies.com
www.3amstrategies.com

Phyllis Wilson, MS

Phyllis Wilson, M.S., has more than twenty years experience in the areas of human resource and best practices in ethics and diversity. Coming from a background that included seven years in the United States Army, Phyllis entered the business community at the time media accounts of compromised ethics in the United States seemed to be an almost daily occurrence. She hopes to shed light on the benefits of ethics and values for the modern marketplace and brings a unique perspective to client organizations that seek to integrate ethics and diversity standards of excellence with solid business practices.

Phyllis is currently pursuing her PhD in Industrial/Organizational Psychology and is a professional member of the Society of Corporate Compliance and Ethics (SCCE), National Speakers Association (NSA), the American Psychological Association (APA), the National Black MBA Association (NBMBAA), the Society of Evidence Based Organizational Consultants (SEBOC) and the Society of Industrial Organizational Psychologists (SIOP).

Phyllis also hosts a weekly radio talk show "Do the Right Thing ~ Right." She loves to travel as often as possible from her home in the Houston suburbs. Between enjoying her granddaughter Evan and helping raise a spunky yellow lab, Phyllis is available for organizational consulting, keynotes and workshops.

Phyllis may be contacted at:

Phyllis Wilson, MS Psych
3am Strategies & Consulting
Phyllis@3amstrategies.com
www.3amstrategies.com